Readers Lo

A Heart Without Bor

"I felt like I was right there ...., feeling the heat, the desperation and the total devastation right along with them. There is no doubt in my mind that this book will stay with me for a long time."

—The Novel Approach

"In true Andrew Grey fashion, this book delivers not only a romance but a powerful lesson on the courage, hope and optimism of people in a country devastated by disaster and poverty."

—Hearts on Fire Reviews

Stranded

"A great story of how time passes and people allow their relationship to settle into routine and they lose their appreciation for their partner. This doesn't mean that they are no longer deeply in love, sometimes they just need a reminder."

—Gay List Book Reviews

"*Stranded* is an amazing combination between an intense thriller-like stalker story, a sizzling romance, and a character study which, through tension and drama, brings out the worst and the best in both main characters."

—Rainbow Book Reviews

A Daring Ride

"All the things we've come to love from Grey are there in the print. An emotional, engrossing, and sexy ride is what's in store with this latest work from one of the best authors in the genre."

—MM Good Book Reviews

"I quickly got sucked in by the story and the characters. There really is so much substance in the plot and the people... he doesn't need a lot of extra language to pull you in."

—Mrs. Condit & Friends Read Books

Readers Love Andrew Grey

An Isolated Range

"Mr. Grey delivers a highly emotional story that captures the reader's heart in one fell swoop. This is an author who is dedicated to his series, stories and characters. With each range story, you always find yourself drawn in, breathless until the very last page is read."

—Dawn's Reading Nook

"*An Isolated Range* is a story not of human triumphs but also of sadness and death. This is an author who balances both so well that the reader is left speechless after that last page is read."

—Love Romances and More

Crossing Divides

"Reading Andrew Grey's new book "Crossing Divides" is great escape from all the craziness of the holiday season. It's a wonderful story that is beautifully written and one you should not miss."

—Reviews by Amos Lassen

The Fight Within

"I loved this book, these characters, and this story. Get it today. Read. Understand and through understanding, enjoy."

—Mrs. Condit & Friends Read Books

"This is a story that is rich in detail, delving into the Native American culture and also sharing the suffering that the Native American's still face today."

—MM Good Book Reviews

"This was a very powerful read."

—Live Your Life, Buy the Book

Novels by ANDREW GREY

Accompanied by a Waltz
Crossing Divides
Dutch Treat
A Heart Without Borders
In Search of a Story
Inside Out
One Good Deed
Stranded • Taken
Three Fates (anthology)
Work Me Out (anthology)

ART SERIES
Legal Artistry • Artistic Appeal • Artistic Pursuits • Legal Tender

BOTTLED UP STORIES
Bottled Up • Uncorked • The Best Revenge • An Unexpected Vintage

THE BULLRIDERS
A Daring Ride • A Wild Ride

CHILDREN OF BACCHUS STORIES
Children of Bacchus • Thursday's Child • Child of Joy

GOOD FIGHT SERIES
The Good Fight • The Fight Within • The Fight for Identity

LOVE MEANS… SERIES
Love Means… No Shame • Love Means… Courage • Love Means… No Boundaries
Love Means… Freedom • Love Means … No Fear
Love Means… Family • Love Means… Renewal • Love Means… No Limits

Published by DREAMSPINNER PRESS
http://www.dreamspinnerpress.com

Novels by ANDREW GREY

SENSES STORIES
Love Comes Silently • Love Comes in Darkness

SEVEN DAYS STORIES
Seven Days • Unconditional Love

STORIES FROM THE RANGE
A Shared Range • A Troubled Range • An Unsettled Range
A Foreign Range • An Isolated Range• A Volatile Range

TASTE OF LOVE STORIES
A Taste of Love • A Serving of Love • A Helping of Love • A Slice of Love

Novellas by ANDREW GREY

A Lion in Tails
A Present in Swaddling Clothes
Biochemistry • Organic Chemistry
Shared Revelations
Snowbound in Nowhere
Whipped Cream

FIRE SERIES
Redemption by Fire • Strengthened by Fire • Burnished by Fire • Heat Under Fire

CHILDREN OF BACCHUS STORIES
Spring Reassurance • Winter Love

LOVE MEANS… SERIES
Love Means… Healing • Love Means… Renewal

WORK OUT SERIES
Spot Me • Pump Me Up • Core Training • Crunch Time
Positive Resistance • Personal Training • Cardio Conditioning

Published by DREAMSPINNER PRESS
http://www.dreamspinnerpress.com

ONE GOOD DEED

ANDREW GREY

Dreamspinner Press

Published by
Dreamspinner Press
5032 Capital Circle SW
Suite 2, PMB# 279
Tallahassee, FL 32305-7886
USA
http://www.dreamspinnerpress.com/

This is a work of fiction. Names, characters, places, and incidents either are the product of author imagination or are used fictitiously, and any resemblance to actual persons, living or dead, business establishments, events, or locales is entirely coincidental.

One Good Deed
© 2014 Andrew Grey.

Cover Art
© 2014 L.C. Chase.
http://www.lcchase.com
Cover content is for illustrative purposes only and any person depicted on the cover is a model.

ISBN: 978-1-62798-548-2
Digital ISBN: 978-1-62798-549-9

Printed in the United States of America
First Edition
February 2014

To my now-husband, Dominic

Chapter 1

LUKA KRACHEK felt the plane touch down and lurch forward slightly as the brakes were applied. He looked around and waited. He had understood very little that had been said to him in the past day, so he simply sat and waited. He'd learned to follow the crowd and do what everyone else did. The inside of the plane was a cacophony of overlapping voices, none of which made any sense at all. The plane moved forward again, engines revving, adding more noise to the interior of the "cigar" he was traveling in. The plane came to a stop, and this time he heard a ding and then the clicks of everyone unfastening their seat belts. He wasn't in a hurry, and he breathed a sigh of relief when he heard another announcement about Milwaukee. At least he was in the right place.

The people all seemed to try to stand at once, crowding into the aisles before noisily filing out. He got his bag from the overhead bin and followed everyone out of the plane. Like he had his previous flight, he went with the flow of traffic. With his limited English, he knew to follow the signs to baggage claim. He had the words written on a piece of paper he kept in his wallet, along with other important words from signs he would see. Luka rode down the escalator and followed the other passengers to a lower level. He recognized people from his flight, so he followed them and waited at one of the revolving belts. Eventually, bags began to slide onto the belt, and he looked worriedly for his old, battered suitcase. Everything he had in the world, besides the information stored in his head, was in that suitcase. When it appeared, he breathed a sigh of relief and lifted it off the belt once it came around to him. Now he needed to know what to do.

"Luka," he heard and looked around. "Are you Luka Krachek?" a man said in Serbian—the first words in Luka's own language he'd heard since leaving his country.

"Yes," he replied with a smile.

A broad man with the same dark coloring as Luka walked toward him. "Good. I'm Steven Koalic from your cousin's church, and I have a car outside." The man extended his hand, and Luka shook it, never so happy to hear his own language in his life. "Did you have any difficulty?"

"No. Only making sure I was on the right planes, because I understood so little," he answered. Steven offered to carry his suitcase, but Luka declined. He wouldn't let it out of his sight again. The entire trip he'd worried it would get lost and then he would have only the few things he'd managed to pack into the bag he was carrying with him.

"Then you'll be happy to know many of the people in our community speak our language, and there are restaurants that serve food like home," Steven explained as he led Luka to an elevator. They rode up and then crossed a walkway over the street. Things looked the same and yet different. There were cars everywhere, but they were bigger and different from back home. "I know things will be different for you, but when you're with the community, there will be familiar things as well."

Luka nodded and continued looking around as the parking structure shifted from old-looking to glass-enclosed and brand-new. Lights flashed inside an atrium, and he saw what looked like moving pictures of light, apparently for no other reason than looks. They didn't seem to perform a function, to Luka's practical mind. He didn't ask if there was anything more to it than art, but it seemed like a waste of energy to him.

Steven led him to a small car. He opened a hatch in the back, and Luka placed his bags inside.

"Where are Bella and Josif?" Luka asked. His cousins had arranged for him to immigrate to this country. It had taken a great deal of effort on their parts, and he was anxious to thank them and explain that he would make them proud. Josif was the son of his mother's sister, who had left Serbia when she was a young woman.

"I'm sorry," Steven said softly and then opened the car door. Luka did the same on the other side, and once the doors were closed, he waited until Steven turned to him. "I'm supposed to take you to the church. We were all hoping you would arrive yesterday so you would have more time to prepare." Steven looked out the window, and Luka braced himself for bad news. "Bella and Josif were in an automobile accident. Josif did not survive, and his funeral is today. Bella is still in the hospital, and we don't know if she'll survive. We're hopeful, because her brain seems to be responding, but she hasn't woken up yet." Steven looked at his watch. "We need to go right away. I will take you back to my apartment so you can change, and then we will go to the church."

Near panic gripped Luka. He'd just stepped off a plane in a strange country, and one of the few people he knew was dead, with another in the hospital. He wanted to ask Steven to let him out so he could go home. It didn't matter how bad things were for him there— this was turning out to be worse. Instead, he sat still, staring out at a strange building in a strange land.

"It will be okay," Steven said.

Luka took a deep breath and steeled his resolve, pulling from some inner reserve of strength he wasn't sure would be there. He nodded and kept his expression as stoic as possible. He didn't know Steven at all, and there was no way on God's green earth he would allow a near perfect stranger, even if he was the only person Luka had met who spoke the same language he did, see him break down. "We go," he said in English. Steven started the engine and pulled out of the parking space.

They passed row after row of cars and finally exited the massive structure. Luka watched it all as it passed outside the windows, wanting to memorize everything about his new home, while at the same time trying to digest the fact that his cousin was dead and his cousin's wife lay in the hospital. It was almost too much for him to bear. Steven pulled onto a highway, and they sped up. A huge domed church approached on the horizon. Luka wanted to see it, but Steven pulled off and headed away.

"We will go to my apartment first, and you can change. Then I will take you to the church. Many of the people there speak Serbian, so you will feel more comfortable," Steven told him.

Luka nodded. He didn't know what else to do. The farther they got into the city, the more lost he felt. Everything he knew was slipping further and further behind him. What he'd thought was going to be an adventure had quickly turned into a nightmare—a hell where he knew no one, didn't speak the language, and everything was changing all around him. Steven eventually pulled the car into a driveway and came to a stop. Luka got out, glancing in all directions at small homes set close together with small lawns, all manicured and mowed.

"Is this your house?" Luka asked. He'd pretty much given up speaking in English. He was really bad at it, and the few times he'd tried, people didn't seem to be able to understand him.

"Yes," Steven told him. "I bought it two years ago."

"You must be doing very well here," Luka observed

"I do okay. The house needed a lot of work when I bought it, but I worked on it myself, along with some of the neighbors." He pointed down the street. "Many people here go to the Serbian church."

Luka nodded and followed Steven inside. The home was nicely furnished. It seemed strange because everything looked so large. The television took up most of one wall, and the chairs wouldn't have fit in the doorway of his tiny apartment in Belgrade. Steven led him down the hall to a bedroom and told him he could use it to change. He wondered where he would be staying. His cousins had written and said he was to stay with them until he got settled, but now everything was up in the air. Luka thanked Steven and closed the door. Shrugging off his worries, he set his suitcase on the bed and opened the case. His clothes were packed neatly, and he looked at the one nice suit he'd been able to bring. He had only the shoes he was wearing and he hoped they would be good enough. They had to be—they were all he had.

Slowly, Luka began to undress. He folded the clothes he took off and then carefully unpacked what he had. As he pulled out the suit coat he'd had for years, he carefully unwrapped a framed, faded photograph of his parents. He stared at it for a few minutes and then carefully wrapped it and put it back in his case. He sighed and pulled out the rest of the clothes he was going to wear. He encountered the second and last photograph he'd packed, but didn't look at it. The emotions were too close to the surface and he couldn't think about that.

Luka blinked a few times and then finished dressing before looking at himself in the mirror that hung on the closet door. His hair was longer than he liked, but there had been no time to have it cut. He searched in his flight bag for his kit and combed his hair. He looked scruffy from not shaving, his beard coming in dark and full, like it always did. A soft knock sounded on the door. Luka jumped slightly and then opened it.

"We need to leave soon," Steven said.

Luka nodded and turned around, packed his clothes in his case, and closed the lid. He didn't know if he was staying here or not, and he didn't want to presume. Since Steven didn't stop him, Luka gathered that he was expected to stay somewhere else and Steven had only agreed to provide transportation.

A chirping sounded from Steven's direction, and he pulled out his cell phone. Luka heard him speaking in English, but he was talking way too fast for him to understand most of it. "Okay," he heard Steven say, and then Steven hung up. "You can leave your suitcase here. You'll be staying with me for a few days." Luka asked if that was okay. Steven smiled and nodded. "My sister had thought you would be staying with her, but she has the kids, and I have extra room," Steven explained, and Luka felt better. The last thing he wanted to do was stay where he wasn't wanted.

"Thank you," he said in English. It was halting and he knew he'd probably mispronounced the simple phrase, but he needed to start becoming comfortable with English if this was going to be his home now.

"It's nothing. I'll be glad for the company. My boyfriend is out of town for the next week, so I'll be all alone," Steven told him.

It took Luka a few moments for him to realize and fully register what Steven had said. He didn't say anything and decided it was probably best to pretend he hadn't heard it.

"He's on a business trip."

"Does he live here?" Luka asked tentatively. Steven seemed pretty open about it.

"Not yet, but he's going to be moving in next month. We've been seeing each other for a year and a half," Steven said as he led the way to the front door. They stepped outside into the summer heat, and Steven locked the door before walking out to the car. "Does it bother you that I have a boyfriend?" he asked. "It's okay if it does. I understand that might be new to you."

"No," Luka said. "It doesn't bother me." How could it—the first stranger he'd met in America was like him. He wasn't comfortable talking about it, though, so he said nothing. They got in, and Luka settled in the passenger seat. He couldn't believe that on his first day in a new country the first thing he was actually going to do was to go to a funeral. He'd heard about so many amazing things in America and he wanted to experience them all. "Are we near Disney World? I want to go there someday."

Steven laughed. "Disney World is in Florida," he told Luka.

"Is that close to here?" Luka asked, and Steven laughed again.

"No. It's a long way away. America is very big. We are in the north, and Disney World is in the south. Over a thousand miles away."

Luka nodded. "Did you grow up in Serbia?"

"No," Steven answered as he backed down the driveway. "My mother and father immigrated like you when they were my age. I learned the language from them. They'll be at the church, and I'll be sure to introduce you."

Luka paused. "Do they know about you?" He wasn't sure what he wanted to say. Where he came from, people didn't talk about things like that, and he was having difficulty expressing himself, even in his native language.

Steven shifted gears, and they began moving forward. "Are you kidding? Yes, they know. Sometimes I think my parents like

Daniel more than they do me. He and my mother have this special sort of bond between them, probably because they both spend part of their lives taking care of me." Steven continued driving, and Luka tried to reconcile what Steven had just told him.

"People accept you here? They don't try to hurt you?" Luka asked.

They stopped at a light, and Steven shifted so he was looking at him. "Yes, most people accept me here. There are those at church who don't. But my mother refuses to speak with them, and they get over it pretty fast. For some reason, no one messes with my mother." Steven smiled. "She's a force of nature." The light changed and they continued on.

Luka didn't talk the rest of the ride. He simply sat and thought. His mother and father would never accept him like that. In fact, they hadn't spoken to him in a number of years. They'd found out about Misha and him and that had been the end of everything as far as his family was concerned.

After riding for a while, they turned off and pulled into the parking lot of a large white church. Suddenly, Luka felt a little less alone. The building looked like something he'd see at home and it gave him comfort. Maybe things would be all right after all. Steven parked, and Luka got out of the car. He waited and then followed Steven inside. The interior was very much like churches back home with its familiar mosaic ceiling. Voices, soft and low, filled the large space with a soft hum. The best part was that he understood most of what was being said.

"You must be Josif's cousin," a woman said from behind him in perfect Serbian.

"I just arrived," he answered, looking up and over her shoulders toward the coffin that sat on a riser just outside the sanctuary.

"I'm sorry this is your first taste of America," she said. "I know it's hard, but you're with family now. We have helped a number of others transition to this country. So do not despair. Say good-bye to your cousin and know that the rest of our family here is with you." She smiled at him and tilted her head slightly. "Afterwards, if you like, I can introduce you to my daughter. She's about your age and single."

Luka was too speechless to move. Mothers the world over were all the same. His own mother had worked tirelessly until his sister had finally gotten married. Of course, he'd disappointed them by not only staying single, but…. He pushed the thought from his mind. He had enough challenges today; he didn't need more.

The woman drifted away, greeting others as they came in and taking charge of the flow past the coffin. He wondered if she was Steven's mother, but Steven was speaking in hushed tones to another woman across the room. Luka wandered around, slowly making a circle and then doing it again. Most people seemed to either ignore him, or were just caught up enough in their own business that they weren't paying attention. He saw his aunt and uncle. They greeted him and talked for a few minutes, and then Luka found himself alone again.

"Hello," a soft male voice said from next to him as Luka stared out one of the windows.

"Hello. I'm Luka, Josif's cousin. I just arrived from Belgrade today."

The man nodded and smiled. "I'm Peter Montgomery. Josif and Bella were—are—friends of mine," he said in perfect Serbian, which was surprising given that Peter looked anything but Serbian with his blue eyes, light hair, and ruby-red lips that captured Luka's attention for a few seconds. Then Luka forced himself to look away. "We met when I helped them learn English a few years ago."

"You're a teacher?" Luka asked.

"Yes and no," Peter answered, waving one hand back and forth. "I'm a social worker, but in the evenings I help people learn English. It started with a young couple I was helping out. Then I began holding regular classes for other people who wanted to improve their skills. Soon I was teaching a lot of people. I taught them English, and they taught me Serbian." Peter blushed adorably. "I learn languages very quickly. I speak a number of them, including Spanish and German."

"I only speak Serbian and German," Luka said. "I took English in school but that was long ago."

"We can change that if you wish," Peter told him.

Luka wanted to hear more, but people began making their way into the church, so he followed and sat down near the front.

The service started, and Luka was thrilled. There were some differences from what he was used to, but it was conducted in his language. Everything about the Mass was familiar and surprisingly calming, even if it was a funeral. He hadn't seen his cousins since they'd visited Belgrade a number of years earlier, but he still felt their loss. Luka had been looking forward to seeing his extended family again. But honestly, it was hard for him to think of much other than what he was going to do now. He knew it seemed selfish, but....

Rather than dwell on the funeral and his own precarious position, Luka let the familiarity of the service calm him. There were people here who understood him. Yes, he was a stranger in a strange land, but he'd found a small piece of home here, and he could live with that. As the service continued, he listened and responded at familiar points in the liturgy, one constant in a sea of life changes.

At the end of the service, there were few dry eyes. It pleased Luka to know his cousin was that well liked and cared about. They prayed for Bella as well, sending her their thoughts and well wishes for a speedy recovery. Then, slowly, people stood and began filing out, talking softly as they moved. Luka followed behind the others, a little lost in his own world.

"Excuse me," he mumbled when he bumped into someone.

"It's all right." It was Peter, and he turned to smile at him. "Are you going to the luncheon?"

Luka nodded. He guessed he was. He saw Steven, who seemed to be following the crowd, so Luka did the same.

"Was the service similar to those back home?"

"Yes," Luka said. "It was very comforting and nice. I'm glad my cousin was so well liked."

"Your cousin was loved," Peter told him. "He was always willing to help others. People relied on Josif, and he'll be missed." Peter motioned him forward, and they went into a large hall where tables and chairs had been set up. Everyone gathered and talked, taking places at the tables. Luka sat next to Steven, and Peter sat on the other side of him. More than once while they waited for the others to gather, Luka caught himself glancing at Peter, wondering what was behind the sadness he saw in those huge blue eyes.

Something in Luka's heart told him it wasn't from the funeral today. It was much deeper than the loss of a friend. Whatever had happened to Peter had touched and maybe even scarred his soul. Luka shivered and looked away.

"You should see if Peter can help you learn English," Steven said from the other side of him. "I was told you already have a job, and that's great, but learning English will help you get along outside of the Serbian community."

"Of course," Peter said, and Luka turned toward him in time to catch his smile. "I'll be happy to help you if you want."

It was probably too soon for Luka to be making decisions, but he found himself nodding anyway.

"What did you do for a living in Serbia?" Peter asked.

The room quieted before Luka could answer, and the priest stood up at one end of the room. Everyone bowed their heads, and the priest said a blessing. Then people began getting up. Luka followed the others, and when the time came, he filled his plate and returned to his seat. Some of the dishes were familiar, but many were strange. He took a little of everything, even the green stuff with white things suspended in it.

"You're brave," Peter told him, indicating the green, wiggly stuff.

Luka didn't know what Peter meant until he tried the green stuff. It was sweet, chewy, and terrible. He swallowed and pushed it to the side. His mother had always taught him never to waste food, but in this case he was most definitely going to make an exception. If this was an example of American food, then Americans were certainly strange.

"That's Jell-O salad," Peter told him in a combination of English and Serbian. "Beware," he added with a warm smile.

Luka wanted to laugh, but wasn't sure it was appropriate, so he returned the smile and began eating again. As soon as he took the first bite of real food, his appetite kicked in and he began to eat quickly, his empty stomach demanding attention. The food was better than the green stuff, some of it familiar, like the sausages, called cevaps, similar to what his mother made.

"You didn't tell me what you did," Peter said from next to him.

"I worked in scientific research for the government," Luka explained, but he gave no further details. His previous employer had not been particularly pleased with his decision to leave, and with the way he'd felt he had to leave, he knew he wouldn't be readily allowed to return. "I really can't talk about it." Secrecy had become a habit he couldn't easily break.

"Is that the kind of work you'll be doing here?" Peter asked.

"I work for university here," Luka said in English. "Josif help me," he added. He hoped he still had the job and remembered the papers safely tucked in the bottom of the bag he'd carried with him. "I have papers."

"Excellent. It sounds like you had some excitement getting out of Serbia."

Luka nodded. "It is free except when the government no want it to be." He wasn't sure if he made sense, but Peter nodded, and Luka smiled.

"Your English is pretty good."

"I learn in school, but not use much. I know is bad." It sounded bad to his ears, but he forced himself to continue. He needed to get used to the language. Everything was, of course, much easier for him to say in Serbian.

"No, it's not. You just need practice," Peter said in Serbian. "First you need to begin to understand, and then you'll feel more comfortable speaking. It's very natural and something I've helped a lot of people with. I can help you too."

"Okay," Luka agreed. He'd been in America just a few hours and he'd already met someone who might be a friend. Maybe two someones, if Steven turned out to be as nice as Luka hoped. It would be nice to have a friend who was like him, though here it didn't seem to be a big deal.

"Where are you staying?"

"For tonight I'm staying with Steven, but after that I don't know. Josif and Bella had written me to say that they had a small apartment I could live in, but with Josif...." He hesitated, then said, "With Josif gone, I don't know what is going to happen." He swallowed hard and returned to his food. It gave him something to concentrate on other than the people he'd lost and how alone he was. Luka turned to Steven. "Can I see Bella?"

Steven paused for a few seconds before nodding. Then he went on to explain that she was in a special area of the hospital and only family could see her. Since Luka was a relative, that shouldn't be a problem, but Steven wouldn't be able to go in with him.

"I can take him," Peter interjected. "I have nothing else to do this afternoon. I'll take him from here to the hospital, and bring him back to your house afterwards."

"Thanks," Steven said. "I have things I have to get done this afternoon. That would be great." He smiled and then added, "I don't have plans for this evening, so we can talk then and I'll show you around if you like."

"Thank you," Luka said. "That would be nice."

They finished eating, and people sat around, talking. Then, after a while, they began to leave. Luka looked around, wondering what would happen next. A few people stopped by to introduce themselves. Some were cousins and more distant relatives he hadn't ever met. They seemed happy to see him. Some spoke Serbian and some didn't, but all of them shook his hand vigorously.

"We can go see Bella when you're ready," Peter told him once more people filtered out.

He nodded.

Steven and Peter talked briefly, and then Luka followed Peter out to his car. It was older than Steven's and looked more like the cars Luka was used to seeing at home. Peter unlocked the door, and Luka got in. The July heat from inside the car hit him like air from an oven. Peter got in and started the engine. They rolled down the windows to let the heat out, and Peter pulled out of the parking lot and onto the street.

Luka tried to follow where they were going out of habit, but gave up after a few minutes and just rode. After making a number of turns, they turned into a huge complex of buildings. Peter parked, led him inside, and spoke to the people at the desk. Luka stood back and waited, understanding very little. Eventually, Peter seemed to get what he wanted and motioned for Luka to come with him.

They wound through hallway after hallway. The place reminded Luka of the labyrinthine research lab he'd worked in before leaving Serbia. They rode up in an elevator and went down more hallways. How Peter knew where they were going was beyond him. Eventually they approached a desk. Peter spoke to one of the women behind the desk, and she pointed down the hallway.

Peter led him down. Luka paused in the doorway, looking inside. He saw an older-looking Bella lying silently on the bed.

"She hasn't woken up since the accident," Peter told him. One of the nurses passed by them and went into the room, where she checked the tubes and changed a few things out. "It's okay to go in," Peter said.

Luka couldn't move. He just stared at Bella. Finally he moved into the room and stepped closer to the bed. There were machines helping her breathe and monitors that showed her heartbeat. He couldn't read them, but he didn't have to to know things were pretty bad.

"Is there any hope for her?" Luka asked.

Peter shrugged, and the nurse looked at him blankly, not understanding. Peter translated for the nurse. He assumed Peter was explaining who he was. They talked back and forth, and Luka managed to screw up his courage enough that he could approach the bed. Bella was pale and unmoving. Luka sniffed softly as he remembered all the energy and vitality that had surrounded her when they'd met in Belgrade.

"Luka," Peter said from behind him, and he turned. "The nurse says there's always hope. There are tests they can do to see if she's still inside."

Luka turned back to Bella, took her hand, and held it softly. He didn't need a test to feel that she was still there. That spark of energy hadn't gone out completely yet. Under his breath, Luka sent her all the energy he could, telling her how much she was needed and that she must come back to them.

How long he stayed there, Luka wasn't sure. But by the time he turned back around, he realized how tired he was. He stepped away from the bed and nearly tripped over his own feet. Peter caught him and gently steadied him. "We should go," he said, and Luka nodded. Everything was so overwhelming.

Luka let Peter help him out of the room. Once in the hallway again, he took a deep breath and got his feet under him. Then he slowly followed Peter back through the hallways and outside into the fresh air.

He rode in silence back to Steven's house, a million thoughts running through his mind. When they got there, Steven greeted them and ushered Luka inside. Peter and Steven talked, but Luka simply stared at the pictures on Steven's living room wall. He almost couldn't deal with everything that was happening. His first day in a new country, and he'd had to attend a funeral and visit his cousin in the hospital.

As Peter and Steven continued to talk back and forth, Luka got the gist of the conversation—they were worried about him. They ended their conversation, and Peter approached him.

"It will be all right," Peter told him. "Things will get better."

Luka wanted to believe him, but everything was so strange. He realized he should have been more prepared for things to be different. He'd been counting on Josif and Bella to be able to help him, but now that wouldn't happen. Josif was gone, and Bella could very possibly follow. Luka was alone, and while people would help him, he was still on his own. He would need to figure out how to survive here. He was a man, and while it was nice of Steven to give him a temporary place to live, Luka needed to start his job, find his own place, and learn to rely on himself in this strange country.

Peter handed him a piece of paper. "This is my phone number. Call me when you've had a chance to think, and I'll be happy to work with you on your language skills."

Luka nodded and accepted the page without really looking. "Thank you."

"It will get better. I promise," Peter said.

Once again Luka nodded, because he didn't have the will or the energy to argue. He stood and shook Peter's hand, then watched him leave. *It will get better.*

Chapter 2

IT DIDN'T. At least not right away. Bella remained the same for days. Steven was nice enough to take him to the hospital each evening for a little while. Luka sat with her and willed her to get better. He understood very little of what was said but could tell nonetheless that people were beginning to give up hope. Then, finally, after four days, there was improvement. Bella began to move her hand. She hadn't woken up, but she was moving. Steven told him the hospital people had said that was a good sign.

The people at Marquette University weren't prepared for Luka's low level of English skills. They were nice about it and didn't take away his job, but Luka knew if he was to contribute, he needed to learn English as quickly as possible. So he'd called Peter and arranged to meet him at a restaurant near where Steven lived. It was Serbian, but Luka had never eaten there and was looking forward to it. One area of real progress was that he'd figured out the bus system, so he could at least get around. He arrived and saw Peter waiting for him.

"Hello," Peter said in English.

"Hello," Luka said hesitantly. "How you?"

"How are you?" Peter corrected lightly. "I'm fine. Did you have a good week at work?"

It took Luka a few seconds to translate the words. "It was good," he answered. "I am… learning… knowing the people I work with."

"Good," Peter said. "It's good that you're getting to know people." Peter pulled open the door, and Luka went inside the restaurant. Luka greeted the host in Serbian and was pleased to get a response. Peter asked for a table for them, and they were led through the restaurant. Once seated, they were handed menus and then left alone. "What I'd like to propose is that we speak in English tonight. I need to really be able to evaluate your skills."

"Okay," Luka answered. "I try."

"The language will come much easier when you hear it and use it. If you have trouble, I'll help you, but the more you speak and listen, the easier progress will come."

Luka opened the menu and looked it over. At least he knew what the dishes were, and his stomach rumbled at the thought of food from back home. He scanned it and found exactly what he wanted. "I have… a burek."

"I'll have a burek," Peter corrected. "Or 'I will have a burek.'"

The waiter approached their table.

"I'll have a burek," Luka told him.

"Beef or spinach?" the waiter asked.

Luka consulted the menu. He chose the beef, and when the waiter smiled, Luka handed him his menu. Peter conversed with the server for a few moments, and then he left after Peter ordered a burek as well.

"I ordered some wine to go with dinner," Peter said, and soon the server returned with a bottle, opened it, and poured them each a glass.

"Thank you," Luka said. There were so many things he wanted to ask, but they were beyond his abilities. Finally he broke down and switched to Serbian. "How will you teach me English?"

"We'll meet a few nights a week," Peter answered him in English. "I have materials we will use. Do you have a place to live? Or are you still at Steven's?"

"I have an apartment. The priest said I should move into where Josif and Bella wanted me to for now. She is getting better. She moved her hand, and today her eyelids fluttered. I know she will wake up soon," Luka said in rapid Serbian.

"Okay, let's slow down. I know it's much easier to say what you want in Serbian because that's how you think, but try English first. Do you have your address?"

That, Luka understood. "Yes, I write it down." He fished in his pocket and handed a piece of paper to Peter.

"Then I will come there at seven on Tuesdays and Thursdays, and we'll work together. You will also need to work on your own on the other nights, and I will give you exercises to help you. Is that okay?"

"Yes," Luka answered. He had to improve his skills—quickly. In the genetics department at Marquette, only one other person spoke Serbian—one of the lab assistants whose parents had immigrated. They had assigned her to him to help facilitate his work, but that meant whenever he needed to speak with his colleagues, his assistant had to translate. Luka knew that would work temporarily, but once he was settled and really got down to the work he'd been hired to perform, that would become nearly impossible. Josif had also been a researcher at the university and had gone out on a limb to help him get this chance at a new life. Josif had written that the university had been looking for someone with Luka's specific knowledge and experience, but Luka was sure it was Josif who had convinced the university to give him this chance sight unseen. He needed to prove himself quickly. "I will work hard," he said in English and received a smile.

"Very good. That was perfect," Peter told him. "And I know you'll work hard." Peter smiled at him.

Luka's heart skipped a beat. He swallowed hard and dared to look into Peter's eyes. His insides tingled as he caught a glimpse of recognition he hadn't felt since Misha. Luka looked away and felt his cheeks warm as his heart sped up, pounding in his chest.

"Is something wrong?" Peter asked.

"No," Luka answered, reaching for his glass of wine. He needed something to cover. He realized he'd been staring. In the next few seconds, guilt stabbed at him. How could he look at someone else the way he'd looked at Misha? His Misha. Luka suddenly wanted to leave so he could go back to his small rooms and stare at Misha's picture and somehow try to reconnect with him.

But Luka knew that was impossible. Misha was gone and he wasn't coming back, just like Josif.

"Something is wrong," Peter prompted in Serbian. "You've turned pale."

"I'm fine," Luka responded, taking another drink from his glass. "I had a friend in Serbia, Misha. He died a few months ago, and you"—he needed some explanation—"reminded me of him."

"Misha must have been a close friend," Peter supplied.

Luka nodded slowly. He tried to school his expression and wipe everything from his face, but it was too late. Luka knew he'd already given away much of the loss and pain that pressed on his heart.

"He was very close to you, wasn't he?"

Luka nodded. "He was…." He didn't have the words in Serbian or in English. To try to describe everything Misha had been to him wasn't possible without describing how another could hold your soul in his hand, blow on it, and bring forth fire, love, and everything good in you…. That was what Misha had done for him. Now that fire was gone. He felt so small and cold inside without everything Misha had brought to his life. "Misha was everything," he said softly. That was as good an explanation as he could possibly vocalize.

"I understand your feelings," Peter said and then looked down at his plate. "I have never been blessed to have felt them. I was never worthy of a love like that."

"Everyone is worthy. Some of us are simply lucky enough to find it, while others continue searching. I think Steven might have found it. His eyes light up whenever he mentions Daniel." One thing he had learned in the short time he'd been here was that Daniel was a subject that brought joy to his friend. "Steven helped get me a cell phone, and he calls every day to see how I'm doing. Mostly he talks about how excited he is that Daniel is coming home and will be moving in with him." He wasn't completely comfortable speaking of such things, but after hearing Steven talk about him and Daniel, he felt it wasn't as taboo a subject as it would have been at home.

"No," Peter countered. "Some of us aren't worthy of that kind of love and happiness." Peter reached for his wineglass and took a gulp. "Some people have done things that make them ineligible for that kind of love. I know that in my heart." Peter took a deep breath, pausing before more words tumbled from him. "There's nothing anyone can do to change the past, so there are some of us who must live with what happened and know that the kind of love you had will never be for them." Peter set down his glass and met Luka's gaze, the sadness in his blue eyes so close to the surface it felt like a presence around them at the table.

"I don't believe that," Luka said. "But I do believe that I've had mine and it's all I will get." The rule about speaking only English seemed to have been forgotten. "To be able to have another would rob someone else of their chance to be truly happy." Luka sighed and looked up as the server placed a plate in front of him with a large, round, multilayered pie that alternated between a meat filling and thin layers of filo dough.

Luka picked up his knife and cut a piece. He then picked up his fork, the flaky pastry cracking as he prepared a bite. He inhaled deeply, taking in the spices and rich buttery aroma. Their conversation seemed to have died off, and Luka felt that was probably best. As he took his first bite, he watched Peter with his burek and tried not to be obvious, but couldn't help watching him open his mouth and close his lips around his fork.

"Are these like the ones you had at home?" Peter asked in English.

Luka sighed softly, relieved that Peter was letting their earlier conversation go. He hadn't expected to be as pleased to switch back to English. "Yes. But they are...." He set down his fork and placed two fingers close together. "Smaller. This not for one man. Family."

"Yes. I can see where something this large would feed an entire family. I won't be able to eat all of it." Peter took another bite.

"Is everything here big?" Luka asked. He'd noticed that food portions were big and everything seemed far apart. People drove everywhere. Back in Belgrade, he'd walked to most of the places he needed to go or taken trams and buses. The rest of the country was easily accessible within a relatively short time.

"Sometimes it can seem that way," Peter said.

Luka continued eating slowly, savoring the food that very much tasted like home. He'd spent the week trying to find things that seemed familiar in this strange place. He found he needed someplace that felt familiar that he could use as a touchstone while he expanded his world. He was trying to immerse himself in a new language, new people, and a different culture that did most things differently from the way things were done back home. He would never have considered leaving a room and not turning off the lights back home, but here the lights were on everywhere all the time. People drove two blocks to go to the store, whereas in Belgrade, fuel was too expensive. Cars were only used for important trips, and people walked or took bicycles whenever they could.

"Americans are strange," Luka said. He hoped Peter wasn't insulted and was relieved when Peter smiled and then laughed.

"I suppose we are," Peter agreed. "Especially to someone who wasn't born here. But what would an American see and think of Belgrade?"

Luka processed the words and nodded. "Maybe they see it as backward?"

"Maybe, or filled with old-world charm," Peter said.

Luka knew they were talking about nothing, really, but he loved the mellow warmth of Peter's voice. "Maybe," Luka admitted.

"You told me you took English in school, right?" Peter asked him.

Luka swallowed before answering. "I did, but it was long ago." Once he found out he'd be moving to the US, he'd tried to review the lessons he'd learned in school, but he seemed to have forgotten most of what he'd learned.

"There is a difference between learning a language in class and experiencing it in real life," Peter told him in careful English. Luka noticed that he'd slowed down his speech, and it seemed to help Luka distinguish the individual words. "I took French in school and then thought I could go to Paris and understand what people were saying." Peter began to laugh. "I tried, and people were nice, but I could understand very little."

Luka definitely knew that feeling.

"Take your time and try your best to use as much English as you can. Watch television and listen to the way people speak. It will help push the words and phrases deeper into your mind." Peter pointed to his head, and Luka grinned. He understood what Peter was saying. He couldn't make himself understood as well, but he'd keep making an effort. "Surrounded as you are with people who speak English, it will only be a matter of time before your abilities improve. I promise."

Luka believed him. Comprehension was coming quickly, but the ability to make his own thoughts understood was so much harder. Only using English, he felt like a bottle of champagne with the energy of all those bubbles trapped inside aching to get out, but stopped by the cork. And yet he was grateful for that cork, because it also meant he didn't have to talk about Misha or ask questions about why Peter felt he didn't deserve love. That was a strange conversation and one he knew he didn't want to have right now, even though his curiosity was piqued enough that he kept watching Peter for some clue as to what he might have done, but all he saw now when he looked was guilt.

They ate and talked about nothing, just exchanging simple questions and answers so Luka could practice. There was very little behind what they said, yet just below the surface something simmered inside Luka, and he could sense it inside Peter as well. But unlocking it took words, and he didn't have them or at least couldn't use them right now. However, as the evening went on and the bottle of wine emptied, Luka felt as though he was beginning to find them.

When they were full, the server took their plates back to the kitchen so the remainder could be packed for them to take home. Their conversation had stalled a little, and Luka found himself staring at Peter.

"What is it?" Peter asked him as he drank the last of the wine from his glass.

"I do not know. I keep thinking about what you said earlier. That you are not worthy. I wonder why," Luka said. He picked up his glass and sipped. Maybe the alcohol was loosening him up or something, or maybe he was just becoming less self-conscious.

"I just am," Peter said. "I can't believe I said that to you."

"Is it not true?"

"It is true; I just can't believe I said it. I don't talk about things like that very often."

Peter looked around, and Luka felt he was uncomfortable. He didn't know why and wondered if he should have kept quiet. Then a realization hit him. When speaking with someone in his own language, he was very careful of nuance and reaction, each word carefully chosen to express his exact idea, but in English he felt strange. The words didn't carry the same power for him because they didn't feel like his. Even when he said them, the ideas almost felt like they belonged to someone else.

"But I am unworthy," Peter said.

"Why?" sprang instantly from Luka's lips.

"You don't want to know about that," Peter said, and Luka felt the cork slide back into the bottle. The server brought their containers and the check. Peter snatched it off the table. Luka wanted to protest, but Peter shook his head and paid the waiter. Then he stood up. Luka did the same, feeling rushed, and he knew why, but he didn't know what he could do to make it better. He hadn't meant to hurt his new friend, but it appeared he had.

"Peter," Luka said once they'd stepped out of the restaurant and into the last of the evening light.

"It's all right," Peter said in Serbian. "You didn't do anything wrong."

He wasn't so sure of that, but didn't argue. Peter motioned down the sidewalk, and Luka followed.

"I catch bus," Luka said, turning the other way. "Is that way."

"I'll take you home if you like," Peter offered.

"I do not want to be problem," Luka said.

"You're not," Peter told him.

Luka nodded and followed Peter the block or so to his car. They got in and closed the doors. Luka put on his seat belt and looked over at Peter, who turned the key. The engine ground and turned, but didn't start. Peter tried again, muttering under his breath. He tried again, but the engine refused to run. Luka got out and walked around to the front of the car. He lifted the hood and propped it open. As a kid he'd tinkered with everything from cars to appliances. He'd always wanted to know what made things work. He checked around and then motioned for Peter to try again. The car did the same thing, but he was able to listen more closely. Luka peered deeper into the engine and found a loose wire going from the starter. He connected it and motioned again. This time the engine turned over and caught. Luka lowered the hood and walked back to the passenger side of the car. He got in and waited for Peter to begin to drive.

"Thank you," Peter told him. "This car is old and sometimes it can be temperamental... umm... touchy." For the first time, Peter seemed to be the one searching for words. Luka got the idea of what he was trying to say.

They pulled out of the parking space and drove down lamplit streets and past quiet neighborhoods. As they approached the property where Bella and Josif lived, Luka had Peter drive around the back. The garage had been converted into a small apartment, and apparently that was where Bella and Josif had meant for him to stay. It was nice, actually, and clean, if quite small, but he didn't mind. Peter pulled into the empty parking area.

Luka got out of the car. "Would you like... drink?" Luka asked.

Peter turned off the engine and opened his door. The night was filled with chirps and calls of the small insects that swirled up around the streetlight that cast shadows over the lawn and walkway toward the main house. "I have to be at work early in the morning," Peter told him.

"Okay," Luka said. "Thank you for ride." He turned around and saw Peter standing still, watching him.

"You're welcome. Oh, before I forget," he said and then went back to the car. He pulled open the rear door and brought out a stack of books and other things. He closed the door, hurried over to where Luka waited, and handed them to him. "These are some videos, and books to go with them. They help with speech and reading."

Luka took them and thanked Peter.

Neither of them moved for a long while. Luka stared at Peter, and Peter looked back at him. He wasn't sure what to do and blinked a few times. He wondered what Peter wanted, but didn't have to words to ask him. He opened his mouth more than once, but the words didn't come, in either language. A car went down the alley, shining its headlights on both of them, and that was when Luka saw them: tears, filling Peter's eyes.

In that moment, Peter looked so much like his Misha that Luka could hardly believe it. The warm glow in the passing light, the soft eyes, the sweet way his lips curled just so, even the mussed hair. Misha's hair had always been untamable, no matter what he did with it, and Peter's looked exactly the same. Luka set the books on the stoop and slowly stepped forward as if pulled by an invisible force. He watched Peter and waited for him to pull away, but he didn't move. Luka moved still closer as darkness enshrouded them once again. "Thank you for dinner," he said haltingly.

"You're welcome," Peter said.

By this time, Luka was so close he could smell Peter's rich scent. Luka closed his eyes and could almost imagine he was here with Misha, but he wasn't, and that wasn't fair to Peter. Luka opened his eyes again, clearly seeing the moisture pooled in the corners of Peter's eyes.

Standing on his tiptoes, Luka closed the distance between them and kissed Peter lightly on the lips. He didn't reach out for him to pull him closer, though he wanted to. Peter tasted good, and Luka leaned closer, adding pressure to the kiss before backing away again.

"Um, good night," Peter said softly.

Luka took a step back. "Good night." He stood and waited for Peter to leave, but he didn't move right away. Luka watched Peter eventually turn around and leave the yard. The lights of his car came on and the engine started. Luka waited and watched as the lights dimmed and then swept the yard before disappearing, the sound of the engine softening in the distance.

Luka turned around and unlocked the door to his apartment. He then picked up the books and stepped inside and set them on the kitchen table before turning on a light. Almost instantly he wondered if he'd done the right thing. He mentally kicked himself for kissing Peter. He should have just said good night and gone inside. But no, he'd had to kiss him. Granted, it was a nice kiss and he'd liked it, but Peter had seemed startled. Luka closed the door and locked it, second-guessing his actions the entire time. He placed his leftover dinner in the refrigerator and gathered the books and videos, carried them into the small living room, and placed them on the table. He sincerely hoped he hadn't lost a friend. Luka sat in the chair he liked and pondered what he'd done. He wasn't an impulsive person. He was a scientist—he thought through possibilities and chose the best one. He pulled his phone out of his pocket and thought about calling Peter to apologize, but decided against it.

He came to the conclusion after doing nothing for fifteen minutes that there was nothing he could do. So he got up, turned off the lights, and climbed the stairs to the small bedroom under the pitched roof.

PETER THOUGHT for the millionth time about Luka's kiss. For the past two days, it never seemed to be far from his mind. He wondered if he should show up at Luka's as they'd planned, or if he should try to find someone else to help him. It wasn't that the kiss hadn't been nice—it had been really nice. That was the problem. Peter reached for the phone, and it rang before he could pick it up to make his call.

"Human services," he said, pulling up his screen so he could log the call as he spoke.

"Peter, it's your mother." She always had this way of making simple phrases sound like orders with him. He'd long ago noticed that her tone was different with his younger sister Julie and his older brother Vince, but barely paid attention to it anymore. It was simply part of what he'd come to expect, part of his life. He'd tried for years to change that tone in her voice, to somehow make himself worthy, but it wasn't going to happen.

"Hi, Mom," Peter said. "How was your weekend?"

"Busy. I had the twins most of the day Saturday. They're wonderful but wore me out."

"You should have called. I could have come over to help and spend time with them," Peter offered. He loved his nieces, Frances and Justine. They were six months old and Vince's pride and joy.

His mother hesitated before answering. "I do just fine with them," she said and then cleared her throat. "Anyway, I have an appointment Saturday morning with the eye doctor. They're going to dilate, so I need a ride. Vince and Margaret would take me, but I said you could do it. They need time together with the babies, and Julie is taking summer classes and needs time to study."

"What time is your appointment? I have a client meeting in the morning, and in the afternoon I'm teaching an ESL class," Peter explained.

"I have to be there at eleven," she said.

His client meeting was at nine thirty and his class was at one. Peter figured he'd have time to get to his mother's, take her to the doctor, and get her home before hurrying to class—as long as he didn't stop to eat. His sister could certainly take time to help. After all, she still lived at home while she finished college.

"Can't Julie...," he began and heard the sound of disapproval forming deep in her throat.

"If you don't want to spend time with me, just say so," she said.

Peter groaned silently. Why was everything about guilt with his family? As far as he was concerned, there didn't seem to be anything else. He caved, like he always did. "I'll swing by right after my meeting to pick you up."

"We can stop at the store on the way and...."

"I don't think there will be time," Peter said lightly.

"Well, if there is...," she countered in her annoyed voice. "I'll be ready, just in case."

There was nothing he could do to change her mind. With him she was stubborn and demanding, and it had been that way since.... He pushed the thought from his mind as old guilt stabbed at him. "I'll pick you up as soon as I can on Saturday." Another call came in. "I have to go, but I'll call you later in the week." They disconnected, and he took the call.

Peter had a very busy day, his only break taken at his desk while he ate and reviewed paperwork. In the afternoon, he checked out of the office and spent hours at appointments. The department was perpetually understaffed, so he worked as efficiently and quickly as he could. Peter always gave each of his cases his very best and never closed anything just to move a case along. But he also knew that while some battles could be fought, others were a loss. He was also well aware that getting bogged down in one case meant he couldn't help the other people waiting for his attention. Basically, he came in early most days and left only in time to grab some dinner and either head home or to his language classes. Even by those standards, today had been brutal, and by the end, he was exhausted. He called in to check out for the day and then went home. He heated up the last of the burek from his dinner with Luka and ate it while watching television. After placing the dishes in the sink and then grabbing his materials, Peter headed out to Luka's for their language session.

He spent much of the drive thinking about the kiss and what he wanted to say to Luka about it. In the end, he decided it might be best to pretend it hadn't happened and to wait to see if Luka brought it up. Maybe Luka regretted what he'd done? The thing that kept coming forward in Peter's mind was how much he'd enjoyed it. The kiss had been sweet and gentle, but so caring, and if Peter were honest with himself, exactly what he'd needed. Guilt and its associated depression sometimes snuck up on him at the oddest times, and that kind gesture from Luka had meant a lot. He went around and around in his head, never really figuring out what he should do. He had made no decision by the time he arrived except to keep things professional between them. He was here to help Luka with his English. That was all.

Peter parked his car on the empty pad, walked up to Luka's door, and knocked softly before waiting for an answer. He heard footsteps and the door opened. Luka smiled at him and motioned him inside.

"Come in," he said. "I have practice," Luka told him with a grin.

Peter heard one of the videos he'd given Luka to use in the background.

"I see," he said with a smile.

Luka hurried back into the living room and turned off the television before returning to the kitchen where Peter waited, watching him as he moved. "We should work at the table if that's okay."

Luka brought the books Peter had given him the other night and laid them reverently on the table. "I listen to all," Luka said, pointing to the pile of videos and CDs. "I read this too," he told him, indicating the book.

"Okay," Peter said as he took the book and opened it. "Let's go through it and make sure you understood what you were reading."

Luka sat down, and they spent the next hour reviewing the material. Peter conducted almost all of his instruction in English. At times they switched to Serbian for the sake of understanding, but on the whole, Peter thought Luka was doing very well.

"Did you have these topics in school?"

"Yes and no," Luka said. It was pretty clear to Peter which topics he'd had before and which were new. "I remember some."

Peter gave Luka some assignments to work on for their next time together. He also told him what he should do if he decided he wanted to work harder. Given Luka's enthusiasm, he had little doubt Luka would probably do both and then come looking for more. Peter gathered his materials together. "Watch and listen to these again," Peter told Luka. "You can learn more the second time."

"Okay," Luka agreed.

Peter stood up and picked up his materials, getting ready to leave.

"I am sorry...."

Peter paused. "About what?"

"That you no like kiss," Luka said. "I will not do again."

"I didn't say I didn't like it," Peter said. Actually, he'd done what he set out to do and had said nothing, spending the past hour forcing himself to concentrate only on the work at hand. It had been difficult, to say the least.

"You say nothing," Luka told him. "Nothing means no like. So I sorry."

Peter took a deep breath. "I did like it, but that is not the point." Peter spoke as clearly as he could, trying to get his point across, and then he gave up and switched to Serbian. "It isn't that I didn't like it. The kiss was nice." Peter paused, trying to figure out what he wanted to say. "I'm not good enough to be kissed like that. You can do a lot better than me." From the confused and hurt expression on Luka's face, Peter knew he wasn't making his meaning plain. "I'm one of the first people you met when you came to this country, and you should look around before you set your heart on anyone."

"Is this because you think you no worthy of love?" Luka said in succinct English, hitting the nail on the head, as it were.

"Yes," Peter said. "I've never been worthy of it, and I never will be." He turned toward the door and was about to open it to leave when he felt a hand on his shoulder.

"Love is for all," Luka said slowly as if searching for each word. "I learn that from Misha."

"Luka," Peter began. "I wish I could believe that." He swallowed hard, and Luka moved closer. Just like the last time, Peter couldn't move. He wanted Luka to kiss him again, but he was scared of what it could mean and worried that what Luka gave he could so easily take away if he knew the truth. Peter swallowed hard, and like one magnet is drawn to another, he moved forward toward Luka's invisible pull.

Their lips touched, and Peter clutched his books to his chest, silently willing Luka not to stop. Before, he'd been too startled to react, but this time he whimpered. Peter felt Luka deepen the kiss, fresh air, sunshine, and spices combining to form Luka's unique taste. Luka stroked his cheek with rough hands and then he kissed Peter even harder. Peter's body reacted almost instantly, excitement coursing through him. Then he kissed Luka back.

It took all his willpower not to drop the books, put his arms around Luka, and pull him close. Luka nibbled lightly on his bottom lip, and Peter moaned softly and closed his eyes, reveling in the taste and sensation.

Then Luka gently ended the kiss and stepped away, locking gazes with him. "See? Everyone deserve kiss like that."

Peter gasped for breath. All he could do was nod slowly. Any argument the logical part of his brain tried to formulate was instantly short-circuited by the "wow" he was feeling. He wanted to step forward and kiss Luka again, but his doubts held him back. "I'll see you next time," Peter said, staring blankly at the walls. Eventually, he turned toward the door, almost forgetting to open it. He reached for the knob, pulled the door open, and stepped out into the night. He turned and saw Luka standing in the doorway, watching. Peter nearly stumbled on the walk as he made his way back toward his car.

By the time he reached the vehicle, his brain had begun to slip into gear again. He opened the back door and placed the books on the seat before closing it and climbing into the driver's seat. "Damn," Peter sighed, gripping the steering wheel. He started the car and pulled out, heading down the alley and then out to the main road.

For most of the drive home, it felt to Peter like he was floating. He'd actually been kissed, and in a way that said he was liked. Peter had been kissed before, but only as a prelude to sex, and it hadn't meant anything. Not really. This kiss had been more. He'd felt it deep down, and his heart still raced with excitement. Peter decided to let himself enjoy the feeling. He had no doubt it would be short-lived, and the world and life he'd come to know would take over again.

PETER DIDN'T get home until after nine. He was still content and happy as he unlocked his door and walked into his apartment. He wanted to be able to buy a house, and had been saving for the down payment for the past few years. He hoped to have the money he needed in a year, so he lived as cheaply as he could and saved his money. Therefore, the neighborhood outside his door wasn't one of the best in the city. It wasn't one of the worst, either, but it could be rough after dark. Inside, he made sure the door was locked and the curtains drawn before wandering through. Milton wound around his legs, and Peter sat on the sofa. The gray-and-white cat jumped up next to him and began prowling over him for some attention. "I know, I haven't been home much," he said as Milton head-butted him and then arched his back as Peter stroked him. Milton meowed and kept prancing back and forth as if he needed to soak up as much attention as he could get. "Are you hungry?" Peter asked.

Milton jumped down and hurried into the kitchen. Peter followed and opened a can of food, put some in a separate bowl, and placed it on the floor next to the dry food he always kept there. He emptied and refilled the water bowl and then set that down as well. Milton ate and purred at the same time, filling the kitchen with sound. Peter went into his bedroom and got undressed, then pulled on light shorts and a T-shirt. He intended to settle on the sofa in front of the television for an hour before going to bed.

His phone rang as he was coming out of the bedroom. He grabbed it off the dresser as he passed. "Hello."

"Mom said you gave her a hard time about taking her to the eye doctor," Julie began as soon as he answered, without any other preamble.

"I have commitments in the morning and afternoon," Peter said evenly. "Why don't you take her?" He wanted to say something about her sponging off their mother but didn't. It would only make things worse.

"She hasn't seen you in weeks and doesn't ask for that much," Julie said, ignoring his question.

"Which is why I agreed to go. But I have appointments in the morning and a class to teach in the afternoon," Peter explained. "By some luck, I can get there in time to pick her up. Is that all you called for? To rail at me because I can't rearrange my schedule to fit what she wants and you obviously don't want to do on a few days' notice?" Julie was almost a carbon copy of their mother, right down to being a grand master at the guilt trip. "I'll pick Mom up when I'm done with my appointments. You get your studying done." With their mother out of the house, Peter imagined that the only studying Julie would get done would be anatomy. Julie was a business major.

Julie was quiet for a while, then said, "She's driving me crazy."

"Well, the best cure for that is to find your own place to live," Peter said gently. Julie could be like a volcano, quiet one second and then erupting all kinds of crap too hot to touch the next. "If you're on your own, you can live the life you want and make your own choices without someone else second-guessing your decisions."

"But who's going to take care of Mom?" Julie asked.

"She's sixty-six and more than capable of taking care of herself. She doesn't want to because she has you to do things for her, but...." Peter stopped. He was treading on dangerous ground. Every time anyone mentioned Mom being on her own, they all looked at him as if expecting him to be the one to take care of her. Like that was going to happen. He'd moved out of the house while he was still in college, and that had been the only thing that saved him from jumping off a building.

"You could move back and take care of her," Julie said happily.

"No. Mom can sell the house if she likes and move into a senior community. Hell, she could sell the house and move to Florida. It's her life, and we don't need to try to orchestrate it for her." Peter yawned. He was getting very tired and had to get an early start in the morning. "I'm going to go to bed." His family didn't do subtle. "I'll talk to you later." He hung up before Julie could protest or decide to lecture him about more of his faults. Peter set the phone on the coffee table and turned on the television. He watched an episode of *Castle* while lying on the sofa. Milton jumped up and settled on his chest, purring as he rested his head.

This was as good as he always thought life would ever get. He was content, and his cat was happy. That was all he wanted and thought he deserved. "He kissed me," Peter told Milton. "Luka kissed me. He did it the other night and again tonight." Milton shifted and began rocking back and forth with his front paws. "I think maybe he likes me." Milton settled down again and blinked a few times at Peter before closing his eyes. Peter lightly stroked Milton's back as he watched the end of the episode. Once Castle and Beckett had caught the bad guy and put one of Beckett's old partners in jail for taking part in the crime, Peter carefully placed Milton on the cushion, turned off the television, and stood up to get ready for bed. He turned out the lights and walked into his bedroom. Milton jumped up on the bed and made himself a nest.

Peter cleaned up and undressed before climbing under the sheets, careful not to disturb the cat, who was gracious enough to sleep on one side of the bed. Peter turned out the light and lay down, trying to clear his mind for sleep. But all he could think about was Luka's kiss.

THE NEXT few days were unbelievably busy. On Thursday afternoon, he called Luka to make sure that they were still on for that evening. After that, he spent much of the afternoon helping a family, whose rental home had been condemned and was being torn down, find a new place to live. Peter finally succeeded in getting them into a two-bedroom subsidized apartment close to where the single mother worked. It was a good afternoon, and Peter chalked it into the win column. It often seemed like he didn't have enough of those. At the end of the workday, he hurried home and made a quick dinner. He also made sure Milton was all set and gave him some attention before leaving for Luka's.

He drove faster than he normally would, slowing down when he reached the residential areas. He turned down the alley and slowly approached Luka's place. He waited while a man walked down the alley, and then he pulled into the parking area and turned off the engine. Peter got out and looked around. He saw the man, who he thought might be out for a walk, staring at him intently. For a second, Peter wondered what he wanted, but then the man turned away and continued on his way. Peter hurried to Luka's door and knocked softly.

The door opened to Luka grinning at him. "Hello," he said brightly. "I am glad you are here. I have listened to all of the videos and discs." His speech was measured, and the words most likely rehearsed, but Peter was pleased. "Come in."

"Thank you," Peter said. He stepped inside, and Luka walked to the doorway, peering out for a second before closing the door. "I forgot to ask you how Bella was doing the last time I was here," Peter said in Serbian. He figured it would be much easier, especially since he was asking something important.

"She's awake and talking. Her speech is slurred, but she is improving." Luka turned away. "But she's very sad that her husband is gone. I'm worried about her." Luka went into the other room and brought in the books Peter had left.

"I'm sure she'll be all right. She has you here now, and I know she has a lot of friends."

"Yes," Luka said. "She's sad she missed the funeral."

Peter could understand that. She'd been in a coma while everyone else got to say good-bye.

"I see her every day," Luka said, switching to English.

"I'm sure that's a comfort to her," Peter said, trying to picture the emotional and physical turmoil she was going through. "Maybe tomorrow I can go with you when you see her, if you like."

Luka took a second and then nodded. "I go after work," he said, and Peter nodded. "She is happy I stay... am staying here," he corrected.

Peter sat at the table and began to arrange his materials. He needed to keep his attention on the task at hand rather than on Luka's lips or wondering how his arms would feel around him. Luka was handsome to Peter's eyes, with his dark hair. He was definitely what most people would call stocky and not too tall, strong, with an expressive face and eyes as deep and dark as a well. They made Peter wonder what was at the bottom of them, what secrets they held but were reluctant to give up.

"Why you look like that?" Luka asked with a wicked grin.

"Like what?" Peter teased.

"Like I food," Luka said and then laughed.

Peter took a deep breath to calm his racing heart. "We need to get to work," he said gently. They reviewed what they had worked on the previous visit. Peter answered Luka's questions, and then they went on. They spoke back and forth, and Peter helped Luka read out loud to aid in pronunciation. Learning a language took practice, both speaking and listening to it. Luka was getting that, and he was advancing quickly.

"Do you speak to the people you work with?"

Luka tilted his hand from side to side.

"You need to do that more. They will help you learn the specific English words in your profession. That isn't something I can help you with."

"What if they laugh?" Luka asked.

"They won't," Peter told him. "They will most likely help you if you ask them. The more you speak, the more comfortable you'll become. You will make mistakes, but you'll learn as well."

Luka looked up from the book they were using. "What if they think I stupid?"

"Then they're stupid, because you're a very smart man," Peter told him, and Luka smiled. They got back to work and finished the lesson. Peter gave Luka some additional exercises. Luka returned some of the CDs and videos, and Peter gave him different ones.

"*The Little Polar Bear*," Luka read, holding one of the videos. "Is for children."

"Yes. But it uses a limited vocabulary, and they enunciate clearly. The important thing is that you understand what is being said."

Luka appeared extremely skeptical.

"Just watch it." Peter wanted to tell him not to get engrossed in the story, but it was impossible.

"If you sure," Luka said and took the video to the living room.

Peter packed up his materials and made sure he'd left everything he wanted to with Luka.

"You like to sit?" Luka asked, motioning toward the living room. "I have drink." Luka opened the refrigerator and motioned to what he had.

Peter took a Coke, and Luka grabbed a beer. Peter followed him into the living room, and they sat side by side on the sofa.

"Was it hard getting out of Serbia?" Peter asked and then opened his can of soda.

Luka didn't look at him. "For me, yes," he said in Serbian. "I was a scientist at a government lab. We were founded years ago under an old regime, and no one ever cut our funding. We brought in money because of our work in genetics, so they kept funding us. Originally, where I worked started under the socialist regime and continued through the political upheaval that followed its collapse. I was schooled by the government and then put to work in the lab."

"Didn't you have a choice?" Peter asked.

"As soon as I took the money from the government for my schooling, I did not. I had to work for them for a number of years, and after that, there was no place else I could go. I knew too much, and they would not let me work anyplace else. My country has changed a lot, but some things stay the same. Years ago, Josif and Bella came to visit, and they offered to help me leave if I wanted to. They said there were places I could work here in this country and that I could be happy. It took a long time for them to arrange things and to communicate back and forth because my mail was sometimes being read. But they eventually got me a message that I could have a job here and a place to live if I could get out. That was two years ago."

"What happened? Did they try to make you stay?" Peter asked.

"I stayed because I could not leave Misha." Luka stood up and walked to a small table in the corner of the room. He picked up a picture and handed it to Peter. "That was my Misha."

Peter looked at the photograph.

"After he died from a fever, I could not stay anymore. I wrote to Josif and Bella and told them that I wanted to come here. I spent the money to call them, and they arranged for plane tickets and paperwork with your government. I did not ask if I could leave Belgrade. I just left."

"Did you sell things?"

"No. I took what I had in one suitcase and my one carry bag. I did not have much." Luka took the picture gently from Peter's hand and placed it carefully back on the table. "I was scared the entire time I waited in the airport. Then I boarded the plane and it took off." He waved his hands in the air. "I was free. I did not know if they would stop me, but I did not want to take the chance that the plane would be ordered back. "

"What about your family?" Peter asked.

Luka shook his head. "They weren't happy when I told them about Misha."

Peter understood exactly what Luka meant.

"They told me that I was no longer their son."

Peter was sure there was a lot more to it than that, but he didn't want to pry. This whole subject seemed painful to Luka.

"That was years ago. It hurt, but I had Misha and we were happy."

Peter nodded his understanding. "Can I ask how old you are?"

Luka took a swig from his beer bottle. "Thirty-four."

Peter was shocked. He'd pictured Luka as twenty-seven at the most. Instead, Luka was a few years older than him. "I wouldn't have guessed."

Luka grinned. "My parents look younger than their years too. Misha was younger than me, but he looked older. We always teased each other about that."

Peter expected Luka to be sad, but he saw life and happiness in his eyes.

"I was sad for a long time," Luka said, as if reading Peter's mind. "But Misha and I were happy together. We had a good life for three years." Luka paused. "He was a good man," he added. "We loved each other. Now he watches from heaven."

"Do you ever feel conflicted between what you feel for Misha and what the church teaches?" Peter asked.

"I used to. My parents did. But I don't anymore. I know Misha is in heaven and he's watching out for me. The rest is what everyone else thinks." Luka blinked a few times. "I'm a scientist. I think rationally. I haven't gone to church regularly since before Misha died. Mostly when I have, it's for the tradition and comfort rather than a deep religious belief." Luka drank more of his beer. "Have you had many boyfriends?"

Peter scoffed and then shook his head. "I've never had a boyfriend. I've dated a few people, but it never lasted for very long." He drank his Coke and settled back on the sofa. He felt surprisingly relaxed. He was rarely like this around other people. He always tried to be friendly and helpful, but those same things acted like a barrier and allowed him to remain at a slight distance without truly trusting others. He could help, and then he went home once they no longer needed him.

Luka shifted and placed his bottle on the coffee table. "Has no one ever—?" Luka spoke softly in his native tongue, the words soft and resonant. "Have you ever been loved?"

A wave of loneliness washed over him. Peter took a deep breath. "I was. A long time ago. But I don't think I have been for a very long time. I haven't deserved to be loved." He sounded whiny and pushed the maudlin thoughts from his mind. The problem was, they didn't want to leave and kept coming, piling one on top of the other. He wanted to ask how Luka could be here with him. When he turned his head, he found Luka staring intently back at him. "How can you look at me like that? What about Misha?"

"He would want me to be happy," Luka countered. "I loved him very much, and I always will. But he's not here anymore. When I first got the offer to move here, Misha wanted me to take it. He said I could have a better life here, but I wouldn't leave him. He was angry with me at first, because he said I was throwing away what could be the best opportunity I would ever have for a better life. Misha worked in a factory, and between us we never had very much. He said I deserved more than he could give me." Luka blinked a few times in rapid succession. "That was when I knew how much he really loved me."

"Because he wanted you to leave?" Peter asked skeptically.

"No," Luka said, chuckling. "Because he was willing to let me go. He wanted me to be happy more than he wanted himself to be happy. That was true love. When he got sick, Misha made me promise that if anything happened to him that I would move on and be happy again." Peter heard a hitch in Luka's voice. "So I mourned for him, and now it's time I moved on. It's what Misha would have wanted."

"Is that why you kissed me? So you could prove you had moved on?"

Luka shifted on the sofa. "No. I kissed you because I wanted to kiss you." He moved closer. "Just like I want to kiss you now." He cupped Peter's cheek with his hand and gently guided their lips together. Peter's breath caught, and Luka kissed him hard, then sucked on his lower lip. Peter couldn't stop the moan that welled from his chest. Luka's own taste mixed with the headiness of the beer was almost overwhelming. Peter pressed forward, taking Luka into his arms. He held him close and used his weight to push Luka back against the cushions.

Luka held him, deepening the kiss, cupping Peter's head. Luka thrust his tongue into Peter's mouth for a few seconds, and when Peter reciprocated, Luka sucked on it, his lips wet, hot, and the most sensual experience of Peter's life.

"Luka, I…," Peter said, pulling away. He gasped for air and stared at Luka, wondering what the hell was happening.

"Quiet," Luka said in English. "Talk too much." He grinned and tugged Peter into another kiss.

Peter started slightly as Luka slid his hands down his back and then firmly cupped his butt through Peter's pants. Damn, it felt good to be touched this way. His head swam, and Luka must have felt the effect he was having on him because he kissed him hard, sucking and probing. Peter figured his lips would be swollen and red for days, but he didn't give a damn. Let everyone see that he'd been kissed to within an inch of his life. All he cared about was that Luka didn't stop, and from his intensity, he didn't seem to want to.

"I…," Peter whimpered as Luka placed a finger on his lips. He got the idea—talk was definitely overrated. Luka shook under him, and Peter followed Luka's lead. The last thing he wanted was for this to stop. He pushed away the doubts that seemed to swell inside him that this was simply too good to be true and that he didn't deserve this kind of happiness, even if it was temporary.

"Peter, no worry," Luka whispered to him, his lips so close Peter could feel his breath. "I no hurt you." Luka kissed him harder, sending a jolt of frenetic happiness through him.

"How can you say that?" Peter asked. "You don't know me very well." He stilled, sighing softly.

"You do that a lot," Luka told him. "Why you sigh?"

"I told you I don't deserve—" Peter's words were cut off when Luka kissed him again.

"You talk too much." Luka grabbed his butt hard, holding him still and kissing Peter hard. Peter throbbed in his pants and his mind began shutting down. Everything narrowed to just him and Luka.

All his doubts receded and his mind was still for what almost seemed like the first time in his life. He went with the sensation and the affection he felt with each of Luka's caresses.

He could barely control himself. Peter began thrusting his hips slowly, throbbing in his pants, wanting some sort of release. "Luka, I can't," Peter said as he pulled away. "I can't do this here." Luka shifted under him, and Peter backed away, lifting himself off Luka. "This is too much," Peter gasped, running a hand through his hair. "You're too much." His brain had short-circuited, and he forced his breathing to slow down, taking regular, deep breaths while staring at Luka. "How can you not see what I am?"

Luka shifted again. "I don't understand. You talk riddles."

"I don't mean to," Peter whispered.

"You say more when you quiet," Luka said. "Body. Lips"—Luka waved his hand in front of him—"say more than mouth." Luka shook his head and then cupped Peter's cheeks gently. "Let body speak." Luka pressed to him, and Peter moved backward, letting Luka do the driving. He quickly ended up back on the cushions with Luka pressed against him, and he reveled in it.

Peter's mind whirled in happy circles, his body throbbed, and he was about to come in his pants like some horny seventeen-year-old. He swallowed hard and pulled away. "We need to stop," he said breathily, trying to make his brain work. He needed a few minutes to gather his thoughts. Luka shifted, and Peter sat up, moving out from under Luka. Luka was breathing hard as well, and when Peter glanced at him, disappointment showed plainly on Luka's face. Peter slid closer, lightly tugging Luka to his side. "We need to take things slower," he said as an explanation.

"Oh," Luka whispered and rested his head against Peter's shoulder.

When he'd met guys in the past, Peter had usually done one thing with them—have sex. The few relationships he'd had had been one-night stands that extended a few weeks or a month, but that was all. He didn't want that with Luka. Not that he really understood what he did want. Well... that wasn't true. Deep down, Peter knew he wanted to be loved, but wanting something and deserving it were two very different things.

"I think I should go," Peter said and slowly stood up. He turned around and leaned close, kissing Luka lightly on the lips. He knew if he did anything more, he'd end up back on that sofa, and this time he'd tear the clothes off Luka's compact body and find out what scientists have under their geeky clothes.

"You still come to hospital?" Luka asked.

"Yes," Peter said. "I'll pick you up at five thirty tomorrow. This is not good-bye, just slowing things down." Peter stroked Luka's stubbly cheek and then turned to leave. He picked up his bag in the kitchen and walked to the back door.

He waited for Luka and then said a quiet good-night. They kissed one more time before Peter opened the door and stepped out into the night. He walked to his car and got in, then started the engine. He saw Luka wave from his doorway, and Peter waved back, regardless of whether Luka could see him or not. Then he slowly pulled out of his parking space and traveled down the alley.

He passed a man walking in the same direction he was going. Peter recognized the guy's clothes from earlier. As he passed, he saw the man turn toward him. Something wasn't right, and since Luka lived just down the way, he picked up his phone and called the nonemergency number for the police as soon as he was out of the alley and could safely pull over. They said they would have an officer drive down the alley and that others had reported the man loitering there.

Peter felt better and hung up. Then he pulled onto the street and continued home. He wondered if he should call Luka, but decided against it in case it was nothing.

Chapter 4

LUKA HURRIED home from work, walking from the bus stop as fast as he could. He unlocked the door and climbed quickly to his bedroom. He got out of his work clothes, washed up, and put on a fresh shirt. Peter would arrive at any minute to take him to the hospital to see Bella, and he was excited about both prospects. He checked how he looked in the mirror and then hurried back into the bathroom to shave.

He was just finishing up when he heard the knock at the door. He grabbed a towel and wiped his face as he hurried down the stairs. He set the towel aside and peered out the window before pulling the door open. Peter smiled at him, and Luka stepped back. "I get my things," Luka said and hurried to grab his wallet, keys, and phone. Once he was ready, he moved toward the door, but Peter paused, looking at him. Then Peter gave him a gentle kiss. It didn't deepen, but Luka felt better. He'd been worried after Peter had left the night before that he'd pushed too hard.

"Let's go see Bella," Peter said after breaking the kiss.

Luka agreed and locked the door after they left. He followed Peter to his car and got in. Then they headed out. Peter looked around him as they slowly moved down the alley. "What wrong?"

"Nothing," Peter said. "I saw a man hanging around the alley last night. I called the police and they were going to drive through. I wanted to make sure he wasn't here again."

"I see man too," Luka said, shifting in his seat. "I think they watch for me."

Peter pulled to a stop. "Why?"

"Government looking for me, I think," he said as nonchalantly as he could. "I not know for sure." His insides turned.

"I don't see anyone now. Did you see anyone this morning or afternoon when you came home from work?"

Luka shook his head. "No." It didn't make him feel much better, because he knew people could be watching without him seeing them.

"It's probably nothing. Maybe it was a neighbor out for a walk. I might have overreacted, but since you live here I was concerned." Peter glanced over and gave Luka a quick smile. "The police were just going to drive through the alley. Sometimes making their presence known will deter people."

Luka understood what Peter was saying, but the unsettled feeling in his stomach didn't go away. He was in this country legally, so he knew he had nothing to fear from the police, but they still bothered him. Back home they were an instrument of the government and often acted first and asked questions later.

Peter patted his leg lightly. "Let's go to the hospital."

Luka forced his mind off the worry and smiled as he thought about seeing his cousin. They rode to the hospital and parked before going inside. By now Luka knew the way to Bella's room, and she smiled as he walked inside.

"Luka, honey," she said in Serbian and then began to cry. Luka hurried to her and hugged her tight. This happened every time he visited. Bella was still hurting so badly. "They say I can come home in a few days."

"I hope so," Luka told her.

"Half the church has been up to see me," she told him.

Luka nodded. He knew she would have plenty of company and support, but he also knew from experience that it didn't dull the pain of loss. Only time did that, and she hadn't had enough of it.

"But I miss him." She carefully reached for a tissue from the tray and brought it to her eyes.

"I know you do," Peter said as he came forward. He approached the bed and took her hand. "It's okay to miss him, and you're allowed to cry and feel bad about it." Luka heard a hitch in Peter's voice. "You're also allowed to be angry and upset as well. It's all normal."

"I don't want to be any of those things. I just want Josif back." She broke into tears for a few moments. Luka stood nearby as Peter held her hand.

"You've been through a lot, and you know there's a lot still to go."

"I missed his funeral," Bella said between sobs.

"I know. It was beautiful," Peter said. "It reflected what Josif believed and was attended by people who loved him. I know you couldn't be there, but we sent him on his journey in the best way possible." She sniffed and seemed to calm down. Luka wondered how Peter did that. He seemed to make her feel better. "When you can get around, we'll take you out to the cemetery if you like. He was buried with his family. No one knew what you two wanted, and his mother and father offered a place."

She sniffed again. "They've been up to see me," she said and once again broke into tears.

Luka leaned over the bed and held her in a gentle hug, hoping she'd take some comfort. "I know how you feel," he whispered to her. "Losing the other half of your heart is hard."

"That's right, you lost Misha." She sniffed and then began to cry again.

"Yes, I did. But more than anything, Misha wanted me to be happy, not sad. That's what Josif would want for you. He adored you and he would want you to remember him as he was and be as happy and content as you can." Luka straightened up. "He's in heaven with Misha, and the two of them are probably sitting at a table together playing poker, smoking those awful cigars and drinking slivovitz until neither of them can stand, just like they did that night in Belgrade when you visited a few years ago."

Bella actually began to laugh. Of course, she dissolved into tears as well, but Luka saw a light in her eyes that hadn't been there before.

"He'd want you to remember and to see you smile."

"I can't. It hurts."

"Of course it does," Luka told her. "It will." He heard a chair scrape on the floor and saw Peter sliding one over to him. "For three months after Misha died, I wallowed in grief. I figured I was entitled. I'd just lost the most important person in the world to me. I didn't speak to anyone; I drank and walked to places Misha liked so I could stand on the sidewalk and cry as people walked past the crazy man." Luka sat down right next to her bed. "People all over town were talking about me. The people at work stayed away from me."

Bella sniffed but seemed to settle.

"I was a mess. My hair was long and shaggy, I didn't shave for days sometimes, and I forgot to do laundry."

Bella made a face and then smiled slightly.

"See, I was stinky too."

"What changed?" Peter asked from behind him.

"I got a letter from this lady right here," Luka said, tightening his hold on Bella's hand. "She told me in that letter that I was loved and cared for. That I wasn't alone, and that Misha loved me and would want me to go on." He turned back to Bella. "How you knew how I was feeling on the other side of the world, I don't know, but you did," he said, looking into Bella's puffy red eyes. Luka released her hand and pulled out his wallet. From it he pulled a half sheet of paper that had obviously been refolded and handled many times. He placed that paper in Bella's hand and closed her fingers around it. "Your words gave me comfort, so now I give them back to you." Luka held Bella's hand, with the letter clasped in it.

"I can't take this. It was for you."

"I give it back to you. I know every word of that letter—it's written on my heart, just like I can remember the last thing Misha said to me. I won't forget." Luka sat and held her hand, not letting go, while tears ran down her cheeks. "Go ahead and let it out."

"I can't. It's too soon, and I don't know where to turn. I can't let go of him. Not yet."

"You don't have to let go. All you need to know is that you're not alone and that people love you," Luka whispered while Bella continued to cry.

"I just miss him so much and keep wondering how I can go back home where everything will remind me of him. His clothes will still be there, and so will that awful stuffed deer head he insisted on keeping in his office. I hate that thing, but now I can't get rid of it because it was his, and throwing it out would be like throwing away a piece of him." She sniffled again and then rested back on the bed.

Luka continued holding her hand, but let the conversation settle into silence. That was fine. Just sitting with her was enough to let Bella know she wasn't alone and had friends who cared.

"How is the apartment?" Bella asked after a while. "Do you like it? I know it's small, and I told Josif we should enlarge it, but he never wanted to. He always said it was efficient and cozy. Like he ever actually lived there." Her lip quivered.

"It's very nice. I really like it. I don't have much stuff, so I'm very comfortable," Luka told her.

"It's a very nice space," Peter added. "I've been working with Luka to help improve his language skills. We sit at the table two evenings a week and work. The place is very cozy, and in the winter it will be very warm and comfortable. It's a wonderful thing that you're doing for Luka."

"I'm glad he's there. When I come home, it will make me less lonely, and Luka is such a sweetheart." She stroked his cheek, and Luka saw Peter tense. "Are you getting along?" she asked.

Peter cleared his throat, and Luka felt his cheeks heat.

"You two are, aren't you?"

"Luka and I are getting to know each other," Peter said and cleared his throat again. Luka wasn't sure what he and Peter were, but he knew he was interested in trying to find out. There was something about the taller, blond-haired man with his pretty eyes and self-effacing manner. He wanted to protect him. And Peter piqued Luka's curiosity.

"I know this is none of my business, but I'm happy for both of you," she said softly and then dabbed her eyes. "Peter has always been very alone. He doesn't let people in very often."

"I figured that out." Luka was very happy they had been conducting this conversation in Serbian rather than English. There was no way he could have kept up otherwise.

"Luka is doing very well with his studies," Peter said in English.

"He make me watch a polar bear movie," Luka told her, following Peter's language lead. "It for children."

"But I bet you liked it, didn't you?" Peter said, and Luka looked back at Bella, who smiled at him. "You did. So admit it."

"The movie was cute," Luka admitted reluctantly. Both Peter and Bella chuckled, and Luka growled softly.

"I have others," Peter said, turning to Bella. "Maybe I could give him SpongeBob."

Bella stared at Peter for a few seconds and then began to laugh, full and deep. Luka wondered what this "SpongeBob" was. He looked at Peter for an explanation, but there didn't seem to be one coming.

"I'll show you sometime. Let me say that they're cartoons, but nothing like *The Little Polar Bear*. I don't think I want you to learn to talk like Squidward."

Bella laughed again. "Thank you," she said to Peter, holding out her hand. "I needed that." She rested back against the raised mattress. "I need to get some sleep, and you two should go get some dinner." Bella smiled at them.

"Okay. If you need to rest, we'll leave," Luka said, switching back to his more comfortable native language. "I'll come back to see you tomorrow." He stood up and leaned over the bed, then lightly kissed her cheek. Then he stepped back and let Peter say good-bye as well. They left the room, waving one last time before walking back toward the elevator.

"That was very nice of you to try to help her," Peter told him. "You knew what to say to make her feel better. That's what I do for a living and I tried to help, but you were amazing. She's grieving and she's spending a lot of time alone trying to work through her loss, the fact that she missed Josif's funeral, and that she's alone. You knew what to say to help her."

They reached the elevator, and Luka pressed the button to go down. "I just tell her what she told me," Luka said. He probably should have stuck to Serbian, but he was sure Peter got the idea of what he was saying.

"No. You helped her," Peter said. "And it was incredibly kind and caring."

Luka nodded and shrugged. He didn't think he'd done anything special other than speak what was in his heart. He'd never done that before meeting Misha. Now he couldn't seem to stop. Misha had taught him that speaking and acting from the heart with others was just as important as thinking and acting with his analytical mind in his work. But he kept that to himself. It was too hard to explain anyway.

The elevator doors slid open, they stepped inside, and Luka pressed the button for the ground floor.

"Where do you want to go for dinner?" Peter asked. "Do you like Italian food? There's a nice place a few blocks away."

"Yes, I like," Luka said. The doors slid open, and they stepped out into the lobby. It wasn't long before they were in the car and on their way to dinner. "Do you have"—Luka paused for the right words—"things to do tomorrow?"

"Yes," Peter answered. "I have an appointment in the morning, and then I have to take my mother to the eye doctor. In the afternoon I teach an English class." Peter pulled to a stop at a light. "You could come to the class, if you like. It's at a community center, so they don't charge. After the class we could do something fun."

Luka smiled. "Okay," he said. Inside he was thrilled Peter had invited him. He was fascinated by Peter, but up till now he hadn't really been sure Peter was all that interested in him. Maybe he'd been wrong. "That is nice." He couldn't help being pleased with himself. Peter turned into the restaurant parking lot, found a place, and turned off the engine. They got out and walked into the restaurant.

The hostess seated them, and Luka slid into the booth.

"Bella really seems to mean a lot to you," Peter said.

Luka paused to make sure he'd understood. "She is family. Josif was my blood cousin, but Bella is family. I love her. She is like a sister." Luka's heart swelled and ached at the same time as he thought of the pain she was going through. Luka had been there—he knew the hurt, the ache, and the wishing things were different that Bella was doing. In fact, he was pretty sure that was exactly what she was doing at this exact moment. "I hurt that she hurts."

"I know," Peter said. They paused their conversation when their server approached the table. They were given menus, and Luka opened his. He didn't understand most of the dishes and peered over the menu at Peter. He saw him staring back.

"Do you need some help?"

Luka put down the menu and pointed at some of the dishes. Peter explained what they were. He stuck to English, but managed to get his point across, and Luka settled on the veal. They ordered drinks and dinner when the server returned.

"Are things going better at work?" Peter asked him once the server had left.

"Yes. I take… took your words and talk more. They have been nice and help me a lot. Some of them have asked me to teach them Serbian words." Luka laughed. "Mostly the bad ones." Since Luka had reached out to them, he found they had done the same in return, and they were now going out of their way to make him a part of the department. "I like them. They will be good to work with."

The server brought a small dish of olives and cheeses to the table. Luka stared at it and waited for Peter to eat before he took anything. "Do you have to pay?" Back home things like bread were often brought to the table, and you paid for what you ate. Luka actually wondered if they counted the olives.

"It's included," Peter told him.

Luka was surprised and began to eat. It was definitely going to take time for him to get used to the way things were done here.

"I bet an all-you-can-eat buffet will be more than you can understand."

"All you can eat? What does that mean?"

"It means you pay one price and eat until you're full," Peter explained.

Luka stared at him and then began to laugh. Peter was teasing him. He had to be. But he looked serious.

"I'll have to take you to one sometime."

"You are serious? There are places like that? It must cost a lot." Visions of mounds of food piled on the tables flashed through his mind. He wondered how they could make money while his mouth began to water at the prospect.

"Not really. The food is okay, but not great. There is just a lot of it." Peter smiled at him. "Like I said, I'll take you sometime so you can see for yourself."

Luka wasn't fully convinced, but he nodded his agreement. The server returned with their drinks and a small salad for each of them. They began to eat, and the conversation tapered off.

"Why do you work all day and then teach people English?" Luka asked. It took him a few minutes to string all the words together, but Peter's smile told him he'd done it right.

"I like to help people," Peter answered. "There's nothing better than helping someone communicate. In the few weeks I've known you, your English has improved immensely and will continue to improve. I'd like to think I played a part in that."

"You did," Luka said.

"Maybe, but it was mostly you. I haven't had a student work so hard before. Is that how you do everything? Attack it until you've mastered it and then go on to something else?"

"I think so," Luka said as his cheeks heated. "I work hard. That's the only way to learn or to move forward." He ate the last of his salad, and the server took the plates from both of them. "Is that the only reason you… come to see me?"

Peter shook his head. "I…." He hesitated.

Luka watched every move he made, from the way his gaze darted to the side to the way he tugged on his collar.

"This is hard for me." He blew air through his teeth. "I come see you because I like spending time with you." He looked down, and Luka wondered if there was something interesting on the napkin he had on his lap. "I don't know why you're interested in me. I'm not anyone special."

Luka had just heard Peter tell him that he helped people for the joy of helping. At least he'd said something to that effect, but still Peter didn't understand that he was special. Luka shook his head. "Do you not know how special you are? You're nice and kind and you help people. That is special. Most people do not do that. They are...." Luka paused, trying to think of the word. "For themselves, not others," he said slowly.

The server returned to their table and placed their plates in front of them, effectively cutting off the conversation. Luka thought Peter looked relieved, but he wasn't sure. He decided to leave it anyway. Peter was special, Luka was convinced of that, and he took it as another challenge—to show that to Peter.

The veal was amazing—slightly crunchy, with tomato sauce and rich cheese. Luka ate bite after bite without stopping. He'd been hungry, but Italian food at home was very different from this. He wasn't sure which he liked best, but he didn't plan to stop to ponder it now. Peter had ordered pasta with a red sauce, and the scent of garlic mixed with spices reached Luka's nose.

They ate and talked a little. There were times when trying to converse was more trouble that it was worth, and times when Luka felt like they didn't need to speak at all. Peter had said his skills were improving, and he felt they were. Peter spoke Serbian, which came in handy, but their experiences were so different that even speaking the same language wouldn't necessarily mean they were communicating clearly. Thankfully, this was one of those times when it did. Luka's entire being seemed to focus on Peter. He could nearly understand what Peter was thinking with his half-lidded eyes and the way he darted his gaze to him every few seconds.

A deliciously evil thought entered his mind, and Luka decided to use his scientific skills to perform an experiment. He cut a small piece of the veal and slowly raised it to his lips, parting them slightly. He stuck out his tongue to meet the morsel. Luka stopped himself from smiling as he saw Peter watching him in return. He swore Peter's breath hitched for a second, and then Luka closed his mouth around the bite, chewing slowly before swallowing. Unfortunately, the results of his little experiment were inconclusive, so he repeated the actions again, opening his mouth a little wider and sliding his tongue out a little bit farther.

Peter stopped eating and stared openly. Luka pretended not to notice and continued eating, adding small sounds of appreciation. Peter had completely stopped what he was doing, staring at him with fascination. Of course, those were the results he'd been hoping for. Luka began to eat normally, pleased with the information he'd been able to glean and deciding what he wanted to do with it. At some point, Peter blinked a few times and went back to his dinner. Luka couldn't help being pleased with himself. Yes, he'd teased Peter a little, but the man was sometimes so reticent Luka wasn't sure how he felt. At least now he had a better idea.

They finished their meals in near silence. By that point there wasn't much food left anyway, and Luka's mind whirled with ideas. Once they were done, Luka leaned back contentedly in his chair, and when the server appeared, asked for the check. He expected Peter to protest, but it was his turn to treat. Peter had done it the last time. Luka pulled out his wallet and paid the bill when it came. He still wasn't sure about tipping. He'd heard you needed to do it from Sheila, one of his colleagues, but he wasn't sure how much. Peter seemed to understand his problem and whispered the amount.

Luka left the money and waited for the server to take the bill before standing up. Peter did the same, and together they walked toward the exit and then out to the car.

"I should take you home," Peter said once they were inside the car.

Luka leaned across the seat, stroking Peter's cheek before pulling him into a light kiss. "Yes. Take me to your home."

Peter paused for a second, and Luka hoped he'd said what he wanted to say. He knew the difference in words was subtle and maybe it was too subtle for his limited skills. He hoped from the shocked look on Peter's face that he'd said it right. Peter started the engine, and they pulled out of the parking lot. Luka watched for signs of the familiar as they rode and didn't see many. He hoped that meant Peter was taking him up on his offer.

After riding for a while and stopping at a number of traffic signals, they pulled up in front of an unfamiliar building. Peter slowed and then turned, parked around the back of the building, and sat in the car without moving.

"I never bring people home with me," he said softly.

"Don't you have visitors?"

Peter shook his head. Then he pulled his key out of the ignition and opened the car door. Luka got out as well and followed Peter up the walk to a back door. Peter unlocked it, and they went inside and down a short hallway. Peter unlocked the door, and Luka followed him into the apartment.

He hadn't known what to expect when he started his little experiment. Would Peter even take him to where he lived? In his culture, allowing someone in your home was a special occasion. It wasn't done on a whim. He'd also wondered what Peter's home would look like, and he wasn't disappointed. It was the perfect reflection of the man he was coming to care for. Peter's place was warm and homey, just like he was. The furniture was old, but appeared comfortable. When Peter motioned him to sit, he did so, and Luka's suspicions were confirmed. The sofa was incredibly soft and seemed to embrace him.

"Would you like something to drink?" Peter asked.

Luka shook his head and patted the cushion next to him. Peter sounded nervous. He went into the refrigerator and got a bottle of beer, then returned to sit next to Luka.

A growl sounded and got closer. Then a gray cat jumped onto the sofa, walked over Luka's lap, and settled on Peter's. The cat's purr was almost deafening.

"This is Milton," Peter said.

Luka slowly reached out his hand and stroked the cat. He was soft and arched his back under Luka's touch. The cat turned and rubbed against Peter's chest before continuing on and doing the same to Luka.

"He likes you."

Luka turned to Peter and said, "And I like you." He tilted his head slightly to the side, ignoring the cat as he pranced over his lap, and moved closer to Peter until their lips met. Luka instantly deepened the kiss. The cat purred, and Peter moaned softly. Luka groaned deep in his throat, adding his own chorus to the sounds of contentment that filled the room.

A thud sounded as Milton's weight disappeared, and Luka shifted closer to Peter, sucking lightly on his bottom lip. Peter hummed, and Luka continued kissing, waiting for Peter to react. He sighed and released the tension he'd been holding when Peter wrapped his arms around him. Peter held him tight, and Luka pressed the other man onto the cushions. At the edge of his consciousness, he heard Milton protesting his lack of attention, but he ignored it. This was way more important at the moment.

When they came up for air, Luka inhaled deeply, smiling as he gazed deeply into Peter's eyes. Milton protested proudly from the floor near the sofa. Peter's laughter broke the spell.

"He's really angry," Peter told him and then turned his head to the side. "Go on and eat. You'll get some attention later."

Milton mrowed loudly, and Luka sat up. Peter did the same, and Milton jumped onto his lap, purring and rubbing against Peter. He jumped down, and Peter got up and followed the cat to the kitchen.

When Peter returned a few minutes later, he was alone. Luka expected him to have a four-legged follower.

"I bribed him with food," Peter told him and held out his hand. Luka took it, and Peter tugged him to his feet. Luka followed Peter as he turned off the lights, locked the door, and then led him down the hallway to a large bedroom at the end.

Peter stopped once they were inside, looking at Luka as though confused.

"What wrong?" Luka asked, moving closer. "You know what to do."

Peter nodded. "Yes, but…."

Luka stepped still closer, pressing his chest right up to Peter's. He then cupped Peter's cheeks and brought their lips together. He felt Peter totter for a second and then return the kiss. Luka pressed him back toward the bed, using his lips and weight to guide them.

They tumbled back onto the mattress. Luka loved the soft oomph followed by a chuckle he heard from Peter. Then they turned serious. Luka kissed Peter hard, searching for the hem of his shirt, and then slid his hand beneath it. Peter shivered and moaned softly when Luka moved his hand upward, soaking in the feel of Peter's hot, smooth skin. When he reached his nipples, Luka kissed Peter hard as he lightly plucked the buds to firmness.

Peter writhed beneath him, whimpering as he held Luka tighter in a silent plea for him not to stop. At least that was how Luka read it, and he had no intention of pausing. He lifted the shirt higher, stopping his kisses only long enough to pull off Peter's shirt, and his own, as well. Then he kissed him again, pressing his bare skin to Peter's. He soaked up Peter's heat, and Peter squirmed slightly beneath him.

"Luka," Peter whined.

He stopped and lifted his mouth from Peter's.

Peter placed his hand on Luka's chest, rubbing slowly. "You're very hairy," Peter whispered. "I like it." He continued moving his hand slowly, and Luka closed his eyes, soaking up the attention. Being touched was one of the things he lived for.

"I hope so," Luka said. He'd tried shaving once. Misha had been curious how he'd look smooth, so he'd bought the stuff and shaved. It was fine for a few days, and then he'd itched all over. That was the last time he'd done that.

"You're very handsome," Peter said, moving closer. He wrapped his arms around Luka's waist, licking Luka's skin. When he swiped his tongue over a nipple, Luka gasped and thrust his chest forward. Peter sucked lightly, and Luka ran his hands through Peter's hair, tenderly petting for encouragement.

Luka cupped Peter's cheeks, tilting his head upward. Then he sealed his lips over Peter's, kissing him deeply. He shifted his weight, pressing Peter back onto the mattress, holding Peter's hands to still him. He loved seeing Peter stretched on the mattress, everything accessible, all that light, beautiful skin available to him. He wasn't sure where he wanted to start at first, but then began at Peter's shoulder, kissing and licking before moving down his chest. Luka loved the slightly salty sweetness of Peter's skin. With a smile, he licked up Peter's side and over his chest to his nipple. Luka sucked and Peter whined. "Has no one done this?"

"No," Peter said. Luka shook his head slowly, meeting Peter's wide-eyed gaze. The sadness that swirled just beneath the surface made Luka pause.

"How can no one?" he asked and then stopped. He didn't have the words for the question he really wanted to ask, and now wasn't the time to talk about what Peter had been missing. Now was the time for Luka to show him exactly how wonderful he could feel. Luka smiled and kissed Peter lightly before licking down his neck and worrying the spot at the base of his throat, which made Peter quiver like a leaf in the wind.

After a few minutes, Luka paused. Peter kept whimpering, his eyes closed, as if soaking up every bit of attention Luka gave him. Luka sat back and reached for Peter's belt, opened it, and then pulled it off. He dropped it to the floor and opened Peter's pants. Peter gasped, and Luka half expected him to ask him to stop. Thankfully, he didn't, and Luka tugged them down and off Peter's legs. He was magnificent naked: tall, lean, and all of him in proportion.

At first, Peter seemed surprised and didn't move. Luka wondered if he'd done something wrong. "Do I stop?"

"No, please," Peter said softly. "Don't stop."

Luka smiled and slid his hand down Peter's belly and then to the base of his cock. He wrapped his fingers around Peter's length and slowly stroked up and down. Peter gasped, and his mouth fell open in the most adorably sexy way. Luka tightened his grip and watched Peter grab the bedding, but otherwise hold still.

"It okay to move," Luka said softly, stroking faster.

Peter moaned softly and began thrusting his hips.

"Luka," Peter groaned.

Luka smiled and positioned himself above Peter's cock. After pointing it toward the ceiling, he parted his lips and slowly slid his mouth over it. Peter was big, there were no two ways about that, and Luka sucked slowly and carefully. Peter's rich, musky flavor burst on his tongue. He hummed and sucked harder, swirling his tongue around the bulbous head. Lifting his gaze, Luka held still and watched Peter roll his head back and forth.

"I... Luka, it's...," Peter stammered, unable to complete a thought, which was the highest compliment as far as Luka was concerned.

He licked along Peter's length, listening to the sounds of pleasure as they intensified.

"Luka, you need to stop," Peter gritted between his teeth.

Luka paused and let Peter's cock slip from between his lips. "What wrong?"

"Nothing," Peter gasped and reached for Luka's cheeks. He drew him up to his lips and kissed Luka hard. "I want you naked too." Peter stroked down Luka's chest to his belt and fumbled to get it open.

Luka chuckled, opened his belt, and undid his pants. Peter pushed them down over his hips. Once free of his pants, Luka's cock jumped and bounced.

Luka sighed and worked the pants off his legs, kicking off his shoes before following with his pants. It wasn't elegant, but it got the job done. Luka settled onto Peter's hot body, sliding their cocks against each other. He licked Peter's shoulder and then up his neck. "You very handsome man," Luka whispered. He hoped in a moment like this that he got the words right. When Peter closed his arms around his back and tightened them, holding him, Luka received his confirmation.

He felt Peter splay his hands on his back and slowly slide them down. Luka started slightly when Peter held his buttcheeks, pressing them close together. It felt good, and Luka thrust his hips slightly, a jolt of pleasure surging through him. He threaded an arm around Peter's neck, holding him close and meeting his lust-filled gaze. No words passed between them; Luka certainly didn't need them. He could read so much in Peter's eyes it was nearly overwhelming. Lust, pleasure, pain, doubt—all were there was plain as day. Some Luka could understand, but others were so foreign in this situation that they nearly stopped his breath. He wanted to ask about the source of such darkness in Peter's life, but now was not the time. Instead, Luka slowly caressed up Peter's side and over his chest, then tweaked a nipple, watching the darkness recede.

"What you want, Peter?" Luka asked. "What make you happy?" Luka smiled, and Peter did the same in return. They rolled on the bed, and Luka quickly found himself under Peter. He wrapped his legs around Peter's waist, gripping him tight. "Is this what you want?"

Peter swallowed hard and nodded. "Yes," he answered, the vibrations that ran through Peter shaking the bed. "I've wanted you since that first day I saw you at the church." Peter leaned forward and lightly kissed Luka's chest, the moved his lips across until he encircled one of Luka's nipples. He sucked until Luka couldn't see straight. "I know I shouldn't do this, and that I have no right to want something like this, but I do."

Luka wondered why Peter would say something like that. He'd heard similar sentiments before from Peter and had always found them confusing. "I do not understand," he said. Peter slid his hands down Luka's sides and over his cheeks. When he skimmed his fingers past Luka's opening, Luka forgot his question. That was probably what Peter had in mind, and at this moment Luka wasn't about to argue.

Peter teased the skin around Luka's opening, and then backed away before doing it again and again. Luka shivered with pent-up desire that built by the second. Luka whimpered and arched his back, hoping against hope that Peter would go further. Then everything stopped. Luka locked his gaze on Peter's, wondering what was wrong. Peter stretched toward the nightstand near the bed and opened a drawer. He fumbled around and pulled out condoms and a small tube.

The packets ended up on the bed. Peter opened the small tube and squirted some of the clear gel on his fingers. Then he began teasing Luka again. When Peter slid a finger inside him, Luka gasped and clenched his muscles. It had been a while since he felt this sensation, and it was almost too much. He hadn't realized how much he'd missed it. A steady stream of Serbian profanity crossed his lips. He couldn't help it. What Peter was doing felt so good, he was afraid his brain would short-circuit.

One finger became two, the stretch burning and then morphing into delicious heat that warmed Luka deep down. He groaned softly and then more and more loudly as Peter moved inside him.

"Is this okay?" Peter asked softly. Luka kissed him hard enough to bruise. He hoped he didn't hurt Peter and knew he hadn't when Peter returned his intensity.

Peter slowly removed his finger, kissing him once again before pulling away. He reached for one of the packets and opened it. Luka waited while Peter rolled the condom down his length and lubed it. Then Luka felt Peter press to his opening and pause. Peter seemed to be waiting for something. Luka breathed deeply, nodded, and wrapped his arms around Peter's neck, kissing him hard as Peter breached him for the first time.

Luka gasped as the breath flew from his lungs. He was being stretched almost beyond comprehension. Peter stilled, and Luka inhaled deeply, desperately needing oxygen in his lungs. Peter sank deeper inside him. Luka wanted to yell, but he couldn't make a sound. Peter filled him more and more by the second. All he could do was hang on and look into Peter's eyes. Only when he felt Peter's hips against his butt did Luka actually manage to take a deep, shaking breath.

Luka was almost afraid to move. He met Peter's gaze and drew him slowly into a kiss. When their lips parted, Peter began to move. Luka gasped as Peter pulled out, and then moaned softly when he filled him again. The stretch, the slide, the feeling that he was a cave being plugged nearly overwhelmed him.

"Are you okay?"

Luka nodded, unable to speak. He held Peter tighter, arching his back and groaning deep and loud as Peter slowly withdrew from him. He gasped when Peter snapped his hips, once again burying that thick cock inside him. Luka's eyes rolled and he inhaled sharply, relaxing his muscles as best he could. Slowly, Peter picked up speed, and as Luka's body adjusted to his size. Luka found Peter's rhythm and moved with him, their bodies easily syncing to each other. At that point, Luka entered near nirvana. Everything felt exactly as it should. He breathed in time with Peter and whimpered when he pulled away.

Peter held Luka's ankles, spreading his legs apart. Luka stroked himself to the timing of Peter's thrusts, his body already hypersensitive. After a few minutes, Peter released one of Luka's ankles and replaced Luka's hand with his own. Luka gasped. Having his own hand on him was one thing, but Peter's was totally different. He had no control now, and had to take what Peter was willing to give him. When Peter didn't stroke fast enough, he felt deprived, and when Peter hit just the right rhythm, he was nearly over the moon. One thing was for sure: he wasn't going to last much longer. Luka groaned and a tingling started deep inside him. It spread up his spine and settled at the base of his brain before blooming fully. Luka yelled as his release barreled into him, smacking him in the chest like a punch that drove the air from his lungs.

Luka floated without moving. Peter was still inside him, but unmoving as well. When Luka opened his eyes, he smiled at Peter, who began to move once more. The bed shook as Peter drove into him deep and hard, sweat glistening on his chest. Their gazes locked together, and Peter filled the room with soft moans that came faster and higher. Peter pushed into Luka and stilled, throbbing inside him. Luka saw the last of Peter's energy leave him and he moved forward. Luka held him tight as they both gasped for air.

Their bodies separated, and both of them gasped softly. Luka closed his eyes, relishing having Peter in his arms, and let the afterglow wash over him. How long they stayed like that, Luka didn't know. Time seemed to take on a meaning of its own, moving around them. Reality did eventually intrude in the form of a thump on the bed followed by an insistent meow and a heavy butt against Luka's arm. Peter lifted himself up and picked Milton up off the bed and set him on the floor.

"I'll be right back," Peter said and then leaned over the bed to give Luka a soft kiss. He left the room, and the cat jumped back onto the bed and sat at one corner, blinking at Luka.

Peter returned to the room and set Milton back on the floor again before cleaning Luka with a warm cloth. He dried him off with a soft towel and then hurried out of the room before returning quickly and getting back into bed. Peter lay on his back, staring up at the ceiling, and Luka wondered if he should leave. Granted, he wasn't sure how he'd get home, but there had to be a bus stop nearby.

"Is something wrong?" he finally asked.

"No," Peter answered, rolling onto his side. "I was just thinking." He moved closer, and Luka settled in his arms. "I didn't hurt you, did I?"

Luka processed what Peter had said and laughed softly. "You no hurt me," Luka whispered. "Make me feel good? Yes. Hurt me? No." Physically, Luka doubted Peter would ever hurt him, but Peter's reticence and the way he seemed to doubt everything had the potential to hurt them both very badly. Luka maneuvered for a kiss and received one. Then they separated and moved apart slightly. Milton jumped back on the bed and thankfully settled at the foot.

"Was this the first time… since Misha?" Peter asked.

"No," Luka answered. "I was with a friend. He wanted to comfort and…." Luka tried to come up with the words to describe what he'd been going through at the time, but he couldn't seem to find them in Serbian, let alone English. "But it was only one time."

"It's been a while for me," Peter said and then pulled Luka to him. "It was wonderful."

Luka sighed softly. He'd been starting to wonder if he'd done something wrong. After the near mind-blowing experience they'd had, Luka hadn't been able to come up with anything that could be wrong, but he'd still wondered.

"In the morning, I'll take you home before my first appointment." Peter stilled. "I'm sorry. I should have asked you to stay instead of presuming you would."

Luka smiled and gently rubbed Peter's arm. "I'll stay with you," he said drowsily. He closed his eyes and listened to Peter's soft breathing and Milton's louder purring. Peter rolled over and spooned to his back. Luka pressed back against him and let sleep start to overtake him. It had been a good day. Bella was doing better, and he'd just had an amazing experience with Peter.

"Why is it that when I'm happiest, I keep waiting for it to end?" Peter asked in a whisper.

Luka didn't know what to say.

"I know I shouldn't, but sometimes I can't help it."

"Take the happy things when you get them," Luka said in Serbian. "Bad things happen to everyone, not just you. If you worry too much, then the good is lost." Luka waited for Peter to say something else, but he became quiet, and Luka eventually fell asleep.

Chapter 5

"GOD, IS that the time?" Peter said as he glanced at the clock beside his bed. He pushed back the covers and jumped out of the bed. Milton bounded onto the floor, calling for his breakfast. Peter turned as Luka stirred, sitting up and rubbing his eyes.

"What happened?" he asked in sleep-accented Serbian.

"I overslept and have to be at my appointment in less than half an hour." Peter rushed to pull out fresh clothes and then raced to the bathroom. He shaved and brushed his teeth before hurrying back into his bedroom to dress. Luka sat on the edge of the bed, yawning and looking confused. He'd already pulled on his pants and his shirt was draped over his lap. At the sight, Peter paused. "I won't have time to take you home and make my appointment. You're welcome to come with me if you want." Peter stifled a yawn. "I'll get you a toothbrush, and you can use my electric shaver if you want." Peter hurried back to the bathroom and set out the supplies. Then he went back into the bedroom to finish getting ready while Luka used the bathroom.

By the time he was dressed, Luka had rejoined him in the bedroom. Peter got Luka a fresh shirt and apologized profusely as they both hurried out the door.

"I could take the bus," Luka offered as they walked toward the car.

"You can if you want," Peter said. "You were going to come to the class this afternoon, though, weren't you?"

Luka nodded and paused, looking around before following Peter to the car. He got in, apparently having made up his mind. Peter got in as well and programmed the address of his client into the GPS and got ready to go. He followed the voice to one of the poorer neighborhoods and parked in front of the house, in the shade of a large tree. He checked the address against what he'd been given. He lowered the windows before staring once again at the half-boarded-up house.

Peter told Luka he wouldn't be long and picked his way up the front walk. He carefully made his way across the porch and knocked on the front door. "They ain't there," a man called from the house next door. Peter turned toward the man. "They left last week." A skinny man in a T-shirt that had once been white looked back at him. "There ain't nobody there except the bangers, and even they didn't stay long. They supposed to tear that place down, but it's gonna fall on its own."

"Do you know where Mrs. Rivers went?" Peter had been working with her to find a place she could afford and he'd finally located one. But it looked like he was too late.

"I surely don't," he said.

Peter nodded and cautiously stepped off the porch, not breathing again until he was on what was left of the concrete walk. As bad as it was, at least it didn't seem like a hazard.

"Thank you," Peter called as he approached the car. He waved to the man and got inside.

"No one there?" Luka asked.

Peter sighed. "They moved already." He wished she had called him to let him know he didn't have to keep working on finding them a place to live. But that was par for the course with his job. People seemed to move in and out of the system. He hoped Mrs. Rivers contacted him eventually so he could make sure she was okay, but for now there was nothing he could do. "Would you like to get something to eat?" he asked, checking his watch. "I could try to take you home if you wanted. I have to pick up my mother in just under an hour."

Luka perked up. "Let's eat. Then I meet your mother." He seemed inordinately pleased, and Peter didn't go into why meeting his mother was not something to be excited about.

"Okay, it's your funeral," he quipped and pulled out onto the street. He drove to a bagel shop, and they went inside and had breakfast. They were done in plenty of time for him to make the drive to Mequon, pulling into the driveway of his mother's ranch-style home a few minutes early. He opened his car door to get out when his mother came out the front door of the house, pulled it closed, and locked it. She walked around the car without saying a word, and stopped when she saw Luka in the passenger seat.

Luka had just opened his door when his mother pulled open the door to the backseat and got inside. The entire car rocked when his slight mother slammed the door closed. This trip was not going to be pleasant. "Luka, this is my mother, Marie. Mom, this is Luka, a friend of mine."

"It nice to meet you," Luka said, turning around in the seat. "I move to back."

His mother leaned forward. "Is he a friend friend, or a *friend*?" she asked.

"Luka is…," Peter began and knew instantly his mother would read whatever she wanted into his hesitation.

His mother moved back. "It's nice to meet you," she said to Luka and lightly took his offered hand. "Peter never introduces me to any of his friends." She opened her purse and rummaged around in it, then pulled out a lipstick. "The office is on Port Washington Road a little north of Brown Deer."

Peter backed out of the driveway and made his way out of the residential development toward the main road.

"Where are you from, Luka?"

"Belgrade," Luka answered. "I arrive here a few weeks ago. Peter is helping me with English."

"What do you do?" she asked.

Peter glanced into the rearview mirror just in time to see her expression. He knew she expected some answer about still looking for work or being helped by the government. He'd heard his mother rail against any sort of government assistance for as long as he could remember. "They didn't help me one bit after…." That was as far as she usually got before either anger or tears would take over.

"I work in genetics research," Luka said. Peter had to stop himself from interjecting. Luka needed to be able to express himself to other people, and his mother was a good test. "I have a job at the university."

Peter smiled at the slightly surprised look on his mother's face that flashed in his rearview mirror.

"I work for the government in Serbia before I come here."

"So you have a good job," his mother said.

"Luka is really intelligent. His cousins helped him immigrate, and they were able to help him get the job here," Peter supplied.

"I can tell that," his mother sniped at him and then turned back to Luka.

Peter drove and tried not to let her shortness get to him. He'd had to deal with that for a very long time now and had learned to let it run off his back.

"Did you go to school in Belgrade?"

"No. The government sent me to university in Vienna. That cost a lot, so I had to work for them for a long time to pay them back. I found out after I'd started that I would probably never be able to pay them back, so my choice was to leave the country." Luka turned to look out the window. "Here, I am… valued."

"Do you miss your home?" Peter's mother asked.

Peter continued driving, watching the road as he listened to their conversation.

"This is my home now," Luka said. "I live here and make a new life here." Luka turned to look at him. "America is land of opportunity."

His mother reached over the seat and lightly patted Luka on the shoulder. Peter swerved slightly and then got his attention back where it belonged. Such a tender gesture from his mother was rare. Peter swallowed hard and turned away, diligently watching the road.

He made the final turn and drove down Port Washington Road to the doctor's office. He pulled in and parked.

His mother opened her door. "This will take about an hour." She stepped out. "I won't be able to see crap once they're done. He always dilates my eyes, so I'll need to go straight home afterwards or I'll get a headache." She closed the door.

Peter gripped the steering wheel until his knuckles turned white.

"Your mother is nice," Luka said.

Peter nodded but said nothing. His mother was nice to everyone on the planet but him. She'd actually tried to comfort Luka, something Peter hadn't known his mother was capable of. Lord knew she never spent her time comforting him. Fuck! He gripped the wheel harder, hoping he didn't rip it out of the car.

"You okay?" Luka asked.

Peter took a deep breath and released it. "Yes," he said. Then he started the car and pulled out of the parking lot. His mother had said she would be an hour, so they might as well do something. "There's a small shopping center just up the road with a great bookstore. We can go there and browse until she's done."

Luka nodded, and Peter turned into traffic, going faster than he should until he noticed his speed and slowed down. After driving for a few minutes, he turned into the shopping center and found a parking space.

Peter took Luka into the store. He let him browse and answered any questions he had. Then he looked through the store himself and found a few books. He found a seat and watched as Luka wound through the store, making his way up and down the aisles. Peter had intended to leaf through one of the books he'd chosen, but he ended up setting the book on his lap and simply watching Luka move. He couldn't take his eyes off him as he stretched to reach one of the books on a high shelf, and just seeing him walk was a pleasure.

After a while, Peter checked his watch and stood up, wandering to where Luka was standing in the corner of the shop, looking through a book of scientific principles.

"I understand this," he said with a grin. "English does not matter."

"Of course you do. Science is like music. It's universal," Peter said.

Luka placed the book back on the shelf and followed him out of the store and to the car. "I would like to come back."

"I think that can be arranged," Peter told him as they got in the car. He started the engine and drove back to the doctor's office. He parked in the lot and got out. "I'll see if Mom's ready," he said and hurried inside. He walked in the lobby and saw no one waiting. He asked at the window, and the assistant explained that Marie would be out in a few minutes. He didn't want to leave Luka wondering, so he wandered back out to the car. He got halfway there and heard the door whoosh open behind him.

"You couldn't wait for me?" his mother said as she put on a pair of sunglasses. "I was on my way out."

He turned to explain, but gave up. She'd never listened to him, so why would she start now? As his mother approached the car, Luka got out and shifted to the backseat so his mother could sit in front. Peter's mother smiled at him and got in the front seat. Peter silently got behind the wheel and closed his door. Without saying a word, he pulled out of the lot and onto the street, taking the most direct route to his mother's house without uttering a word the entire ride.

Not that his mother noticed. She talked with Luka as though she'd known him for years, regardless of the language issues. He even had her laughing at one point. Peter saw Luka's smile in the rearview mirror and knew it should have made him happy, but it didn't. He simply seethed at the ease between them.

By the time he pulled into his mother's driveway, he was about ready to blow his stack. The worst part was he didn't quite know why. There was no reason on earth why Luka getting along with his mother should make him so angry, so....

"Thank you for the ride, Peter," his mother said before opening her car door, interrupting his thoughts. "It was wonderful to meet you, Luka," she added with a smile that made Peter grind his teeth.

She closed the door, and Peter was about to put the car in reverse when his brother's blue BMW came into view. He put the car in park and waited. Vince pulled to a stop behind him and got out of his car. Peter opened his door and got out as well. He was already opening the back door of the sedan by the time Peter approached the car. Vince emerged from the backseat with a car carrier that held a sleeping baby.

Peter motioned to Luka and waited for him to approach. "Vince this is Luka. Luka, my brother Vince," he said, and then turned to the carrier looking closely, "and this precious girl is Justine." He peered in the car, expecting to see another carrier. Luka and Vince shook hands, and Peter returned his attention to his adorable niece, preparing to lift her out of the carrier.

"Frances is home with her mother," Vince explained.

Their mother approached, nudged Peter to the side, and began unfastening the catches on the infant carrier. Once they were free, his mother lifted Justine out and into her arms, cooing softly.

"I have the diaper bag in the back," Vince said and hurried to get it.

Peter's mother was already heading toward the house with the baby.

Vince grabbed the carrier on his way through and hurried behind her. "I'll be right back so you can go," he said.

They stepped into the house, and after a few minutes, Vince came back out. "Thanks, Mom. I should be just a few hours," he called from the doorway and then hurried down the walk and driveway toward them.

Vince said a quick good-bye to both of them, got in his car, and started backing out of the driveway.

Peter stood rooted in his spot. He hadn't seen his nieces in weeks, and he'd barely gotten to see her before his mother had whisked Justine away. He couldn't believe how much that hurt. He wanted to ask Luka if he minded if they went inside, but after checking the time, he realized if they hurried, they could make a quick stop at a drive-through before the class he had to teach. "We should go too," Peter said with resignation and walked toward his car. He could feel Luka's gaze on him. He opened his door and waited for Luka to get inside. Then he slid into his seat and started the car.

Luka was quiet as they rode out of Mequon's suburban quiet toward the freeway. "Why you angry with me?" Luka asked just before Peter turned to enter the freeway.

"I'm not," Peter answered. He should have been used to his family's treatment and attitudes by now. "I'm angry with myself."

"You do that a lot," Luka said.

Peter wasn't sure if he meant it as a statement or a question. Since the statement didn't require a response, he took it that way.

"Do they...." Luka paused. "Do they make believe you're not there a lot?" he asked, switching to Serbian.

Peter thought for a few seconds. "I guess they do."

"Why?" Luka asked.

That was the question, and one Peter didn't want to go into. But it appeared he would have to. Luka was inquisitive and he'd wonder and ask until Peter told him. He was fairly sure of that.

"Why are you afraid?"

Peter continued driving. "I can't talk about this now. I really can't," he said softly. "I have to get my mind around the class I'm going to teach, and if I start thinking about all this, I'll never get my mind in the right place." Peter knew why his family members acted the way they did, but he'd pushed the details aside for a long time, and he didn't want to bring them forward again.

"Okay," Luka said. "But you'll tell me later?"

"If I can," Peter said. He wasn't sure this was a good idea, and it wasn't the kind of thing he talked to anyone about… ever. Hell, that was why he never brought any of the few friends he had to see his family. He continued driving, exiting the freeway and driving to the Esperanza Unida building. He found a place to park and led Luka inside. "Most of the people in this class speak Spanish as a first language," Peter explained, glad to be on more familiar ground. They took the stairs to the second floor and entered a small classroom. There were already a number of familiar students—most young to middle-aged adults—gathered, talking among themselves.

Luka took a seat in the front, but off to the side. More students filtered in over the next ten minutes. Peter brought Luka a cup of coffee and a few of the cookies from the back table, wishing he hadn't forgotten to stop to eat. He ate a few cookies himself, and then, at one, he closed the door and began the class.

He conducted the class almost entirely in English and encouraged his students to ask their questions in English. Sometimes it was too much for them and they lapsed into Spanish, but Peter worked with them to make sure they understood the English equivalent before going on. This class never moved very fast, but his students progressed, and that was all that mattered. Through most of the class, he had to force his attention away from Luka and onto his students. By the time the hour was over, he was ravenously hungry and exhausted. He said good-bye to the students as they came up to shake his hand and exchange a kind word before leaving.

"How often you do this?" Luka asked once they were alone.

"Every two weeks," Peter answered. "Some of them have been taking the class for a year or more. They learn more slowly because many of them have limited education to start with. But they want to fit into their adopted country." Peter walked to the window overlooking National Avenue. "This is the heart of the Spanish-speaking neighborhood here in town. Esperanza Unida is a community organization. They do job training and community support. The restaurant in the building is part of a food-service training program, and just down the street they have garages and other nonprofit businesses that teach other skills. This community has had a tough time, so they've banded together to try to help pull themselves up to a better life. And it's working."

Peter took one more look out the window and then turned back to Luka, who stared at him, his eyes wide, as if he'd just figured out some secret. "Is your family why you do this?" Luka asked. "You help people because your family not help you?"

Peter didn't answer right away. Luka's observation was too close to the mark for comfort. "I like helping people," he deflected. "Let's go get something to eat. They have great Mexican food at the restaurant downstairs." He hoped like hell the thought of food would be enough to distract Luka, and it worked. They had a great lunch, and then Peter drove Luka home. He debated going inside and figured it would be better to simply go home to avoid what he knew was coming.

But Luka had other ideas, it seemed. "Come inside and we talk," he said.

Peter cursed silently and followed Luka inside. Peter sat down, and Luka got two beers, brought them into the living room, and sat on the sofa next to him.

"You want to use English?"

Peter had to. He wasn't sure he could tell this story in any other language. It was too personal. "When I was six and Vince about eight or nine, I guess, we were playing in the backyard." Peter tried to keep his mind clear. "We had a shed in the back where my dad used to keep his stuff. Vince got hold of the key somehow and unlocked the door. We never got to go in there, and I stood in the doorway, peering into my father's private domain. There were power tools and pieces of wood on the workbench. My dad carved duck decoys as a hobby, and I saw some wooden ducks sitting on one of the benches. I didn't dare go inside, but Vince did. He walked in and started looking around. He even climbed on one of the benches so he could see what was on the upper shelves."

Peter twisted off the top of the beer bottle and took a large drink. "I don't remember very much. It's been a long time. But it smelled like fresh wood and linseed oil. Mom hated the smell and made Dad work out in the shed. At least that's what she said." Peter took another drink. "I remember Vince making an 'oooh' sound and then he climbed down off the bench and showed me what he'd found." Peter shivered and looked around, wondering how he could get out of here. Luka placed a hand on his knee and patted him gently.

"It is okay," he said.

"Vince placed the gun he'd found in my hand. I remember it being heavy and cold. I almost dropped it." Peter closed his eyes. "Vince thought it was a toy. He grabbed it from my hand and raced out into the yard, pretending to shoot birds and stuff, making bang-bang noises." Peter tensed. "We heard Dad coming home, so we raced back into the shed. We knew Dad would be mad if he caught us." Peter's heart rate increased and he could barely breathe. "I remember closing the shed door, and then it banged open. I saw Dad standing in the doorway. The next thing I knew, the gun went off and I fell on my butt. When I opened my eyes, I had the gun in my hands and a huge red stain was spreading over Dad's chest." Peter's voice broke. "The next thing I saw was Dad falling over. I dropped the gun and raced to him. Mom hurried out and told both of us to go in the house."

"What happened then?" Luka asked.

"A lot of people asked me all kinds of questions I couldn't answer. I don't remember very much after that. All I know is that I had the gun in my hands and then my dad was dead. I shot my dad. It was an accident, everyone told me that, but none of my family could ever really forgive me for it. I left my sister and brother without a dad and my mother without a husband." Peter shook like a leaf. "See, I told you—I don't deserve to be happy. I will never deserve it, not after shooting my own father." Peter drained the rest of the beer in a few gulps. "This is what I have to live with, what I've had to live with since I was six years old. The last time I saw my father, he was on the ground in a pool of his own blood, and I was the one who did that to him." Peter stood up, and the room spun for a few seconds. He found he could barely stand up. "I've had to live with this for almost as long as I can remember." He paused. "I understand why they treat me the way they do. I cost my brother and sister their father."

Luka stood and moved around the table. "You were six years old," he said softly. "You were very young and didn't know what was happening. It was...." He quieted briefly. "Accident?"

"Yes, it was. But I have never forgiven myself for it, and neither have they."

Luka nodded slowly. "That why you try to help. You try to make up for what you did. You no need to do that. You were child; it was accident. Brother and sister should forgive. Mother should forgive."

His mother was a completely different story. She had always treated him differently after that. Vince and Julie were always treated as though they were special, and he was ignored if at all possible. Otherwise they acted like he owed them something. "I was never good enough after that. Things were hard for Mom, and she did her best to keep the family together and functioning. She hadn't worked while Dad was alive, but she had to get a job after that. I was expected to take care of the house. Most six- and seven-year-olds are instructed to keep their room clean, but I had to take care of a whole house. The others had things they had to do as well, but I took on all I could."

"See? You try to make right, but can't."

Peter nodded. Luka was right. He could never atone for what he'd done, and he would never be able to even if he lived for a hundred years. They would never forgive him, and worst of all, he could never forgive himself. "You're right, I never will." Peter began walking around the small room. "See now why I don't deserve to be happy? I took away the happiness of my mother, brother, and sister. I deserve to spend the rest of my life trying to make up for something that can't be made up for."

"No," Luka said. "You need to stop. Everyone deserve to be happy."

Peter sighed. "Not me," he whispered. He turned away from Luka. "I should go." he walked toward the door and heard Luka hurrying behind him.

"No. You need to stay here. Not be alone."

"See," he began, stopping in his tracks. "I deserve to be alone." He reached for the door just as Luka caught his hand.

"No. You no deserve...." He swore under his breath using terms Peter didn't know. "You no worse... no, no, no... you are just as good as anyone else." Luka sighed and held Peter's hand. "When I boy, I want to go to circus. Mama say I no can go. So I sneak money from the jar she keep... savings in and go with my friends. I eight or nine, and stupid." Luka smiled. "We have good time and when I come home, Mama...." Luka paused and turned around, motioning toward his butt. Peter got the idea and nodded.

"She spanked you," Peter supplied.

"Yes, she spanked me. The money I took was part of what we were going to use for food. I went to the circus, and now we had to eat less. Mama and Papa had less to eat, we all did because of what I did."

"So, you didn't understand," Peter said.

Luka nodded. "You didn't understand either. You just child like me. We do stupid things when young. It what children do. It not need mean they bad for always."

"But your mother or father didn't die because of what you did."

"No. But we not have enough to eat. We all go hungry because I think only of me. I learn. We all learn." Luka stepped closer, touching his cheek. "I very sorry about your dad. He sounds like good man."

Peter placed his hands over his eyes. "The memories I have of my father, us doing things together, were wonderful. He used to take us to the beach on Saturdays, and afterwards he always took us for ice cream or something like that, but we weren't to tell Mom. It was something special that we did just with him." The tears welling in Peter's eyes overflowed and ran down his cheek. "I loved him so much. I knew he would be angry if he caught us, but I never wanted to hurt him." Peter sobbed as he tried to concentrate on other memories of his dad besides seeing him lying on the ground in his own blood. "He used to take us in the backyard and give us airplane rides. He'd twirl me in a circle until I couldn't stand up. I remember wandering around like I was drunk, falling on the ground laughing, and then asking him to do it again." Peter cleared his throat. "He always had time for us. I know that now. He worked a lot, but always made time for us when he was home." The memories he had were snippets and impressions more than anything concrete. He'd hung on to them as best he could because it was all he had that wasn't painful.

"I used to pray that God would take me and bring Daddy back in my place. That way I would be gone and everyone would have what they wanted back." Peter lowered his hands and wiped his cheeks, "I'd still do that if it would bring him back. But nothing ever can." He took a deep breath. "I will never be able to replace him, so I have to do what I can to make up for the good he might have done if he were still with us. I know it might sound crazy, but that's what I feel I have to do."

"Okay," Luka said. "But you no have to do it alone."

"Yes, I do. I'm the one responsible, so I'm the one who has to bear the brunt of the pain," Peter said. He needed to get out of here and back to his apartment, where he could hide in peace and hold Milton for a while.

Luka narrowed his eyes, then took Peter's hand and led him back through the apartment to the sofa. "Everyone has pain," Luka said as he motioned grandly over his head. "Bella has pain because Josif not here. You have pain because your dad not here."

"But he's not here because of *me*," Peter explained once more. He'd had years to think about this, and no matter how he tried to rationalize or try to let it go, he always came back to that fact. His father wasn't around because of him, and there wasn't a damned thing he could do about it. "I know it's hard for you to understand, but I've lived with this every day of my life since then. I've thought about it every way there is, and I always come back to the same thing: I shot my father. Yes, it was an accident, and I was only a child, but I still killed him and took him away from the rest of my family." Peter closed his eyes. "I've wished myself dead more times than I can count. But I always thought that was too good for me because then I would be out of my misery."

Luka gaped at him. "No. It was accident. Everyone blames you, but I ask this: Would your dad blame you?"

Peter paused, his eyes widening. In all the years, no one had ever asked him that question. "I...." He thought about it and realized he didn't have an answer for that.

"Was gun yours?" Luka asked. "No. It was your dad's. He put gun in there and kept it loaded. Did you put bullets in?"

Peter stared at Luka and then shook his head. "We still shouldn't have been playing in there, and Vince should have put the gun back when he found it." How many times had Peter wished he'd never seen or touched that gun? At least a million over the years. He'd never been near one since, and he never intended to touch one again.

Most of the time, Peter was able to keep the hurt and ache of what he'd done inside a box, where he could deal with it. Telling Luka the story had brought it all back, and the hurt seemed new and acute, like the incident had happened just a few days before. More than anything he wanted this to go away, but it wouldn't and it was never going to. So once again, Peter needed to figure out how to deal with the hurt and pain. More than once he'd considered moving far away. But that was only geography, and no matter where he ran, he couldn't get away from his own feelings. They'd follow him no matter where he went.

"I appreciate you wanting to be here with me, but I need to deal with this on my own." Peter stood up. "I really appreciate you trying to help, but no one can." He sighed and left without a word.

He got in his car, but couldn't keep from looking at the doorway of Luka's place. Luka stood there watching him with an expression on his face that Peter couldn't read. He sighed and backed out of the parking space. He passed a man walking through the alley, but barely gave him a second thought as he descended into his own thoughts and pain.

By the time he got to his apartment, he hardly remembered the drive. He got out of the car and shuffled up the walk before entering his building and then unlocking his door. Milton greeted him the way he usually did, and Peter closed the door and slumped onto the sofa. Milton immediately jumped on his lap, and Peter held the soft cat in his arms. Milton's purrs filled Peter's ears, and he desperately tried to keep himself together. Shooting his father had happened years—decades—ago and yet the emotion and pain jabbed at him like it taken place yesterday. He knew this pain, he'd felt it before, but not this intense. He thought the feelings he was developing for Luka had to be at the heart of it. He'd been enjoying the time they spent together. More than once Luka had allowed him to forget, at least for a little while.

Milton squirmed, and Peter released him. He jumped to the floor and sat down, stared up at Peter, and then began cleaning himself. Peter lay down and closed his eyes. Maybe he was just tired. He kept his eyes closed when Milton jumped back up and settled on his chest. He was such a fool. He opened his eyes and looked around the empty apartment. Luka had said he shouldn't be alone and had wanted him to stay. He would have comforted him and tried to help him feel better. Instead, Peter was alone and miserable. On top of that, he missed Luka. "Crap," he said softly. He now wished he hadn't left, because being alone like this sucked.

Eventually, from simply lying still and letting his mind wander, he dozed off. Sometimes he dreamed of his dad. The dreams usually centered on the shooting incident, but this time he and his dad were playing in the backyard, his dad twirling him in a circle until Peter cried that he was going to woof. His dad placed him on the soft grass and laughed. Peter laughed as well.

He started awake. Milton jumped down to the floor and mrowed at him for disturbing him. Peter wiped his eyes and realized his cheeks were wet. He'd been crying, and he was still crying as the last of his father's remembered laughter echoed in his head and then died away. He reached for a tissue and settled back on the sofa, letting the tears come freely.

Chapter 6

LUKA WALKED into the Marquette Science Center and nearly stumbled over a student who'd bent to tie his shoes. He excused himself and shook his head to clear away the distractions. Ever since Peter left Saturday afternoon, his head had felt as if it were stuffed with cotton. He'd tried to think straight, but his thoughts and worries kept returning to Peter and the way he'd been hurting. Luka made sure the student was all right and then hurried on to his small office near the lab where he worked. He shared it with one of the other researchers, so it was a tight fit, but he didn't care.

"Nice weekend?" Johnny Miller asked with a smile. He was young and full of energy and excitement. Luka liked working with him because his energy was contagious.

Luka shrugged. "It not bad," he answered and set his bag down next to his desk.

"'It wasn't bad' is a better way to say it, and I'm sorry," Johnny told him with a grin. "Mine was special. I asked my girlfriend Holly to marry me and she said yes. So I'm getting married."

Luka smiled and shook his hand. "All the best," he said. He wasn't sure if that was right, but Johnny's smile didn't diminish, so Luka guessed he was okay. "I hope you be happy."

"We will be," Johnny said, shaking all over like an excited puppy.

Luka sat down and started his computer. He read his e-mails, most of them junk, and then turned around to find Johnny hardly able to sit still in his chair. "I need help," Luka said.

Johnny looked up. "What kind?"

"I need to find... head doctor," Luka told him. He was trying to think of the word he wanted to describe what this person would do, but he only knew the terms in Serbian, and that would be no help to Johnny.

Johnny smiled. "You mean a psychiatrist or a psychologist."

"The kind people talk to," Luka told him.

"There's a psychology department. I bet they can help you." Johnny became serious. "You're feeling okay, aren't you?"

"It not for me," he said. "Can you tell me where to go?"

"Sure," Johnny said. He opened his desk drawer and pulled out a map. He showed Luka where it was and then handed him the map. Luka stood up and hurried out of the office and the building, then followed the map to the area of the campus Johnny had indicated. The building he entered was old, with wooden staircases and carved banisters that showed the wear of years of students passing through. He climbed to the second floor and looked at each door he passed.

"Can I help you?" a lady asked when he peered inside one of the offices.

"Psychology?" he asked.

She nodded. "How may I help you?"

Luka stepped into the office. "I have a friend who needs help."

"We're a teaching institution. We don't take patients," she said.

"Marlene, is something wrong?" a gray-haired man with glasses asked as he stepped out of an office.

"This man is looking for someone who can provide treatment. I explained we don't do that," she said.

"It's all right," the man said and motioned for Luka to follow him into a much larger office than the one he had. "How can I help you?" the man asked quietly and indicated one of the chairs.

"I Dr. Luka Krachek. I work in science research. I sorry for my English. I just come to this country."

"I'm Dr. Middlebach, the head of the psychology department." He shook Luka's hand and sat in the chair next to his. "You said you need help."

"I have friend, and he need help." Luka thought for a few seconds about how much he should explain. "As child, my friend hurt someone very bad by accident. He tell me the story and I think he not remembering right. It seem wrong, and he was six." The words came out fast.

"Okay, slow down. Your friend did something he thinks is very bad when he was six?"

"Yes. He feels very bad and cannot forgive. But at most important part, he say he not remember," Luka explained.

"Ah," Dr. Middlebach said. "I must caution you that I am not providing a diagnosis or a course of action, but children often block the most traumatic moments. It's the way they cope with things. It allows them to deal with the trauma better." He paused, and Luka waited. "There's also the possibility that your friend does remember but isn't sharing what he feels is the worst portion of his actions."

It took Luka a few seconds to figure out what he was being told. Then he shook his head. "Why he lie? He already say he did it. He think he did it."

"But you don't," Dr. Middlebach said with a small smile.

"I scientist and I must know. He does not know—he only think." Luka paused, hoping the language barrier wasn't stopping him from getting his point across. "I see man use… special sleep to get woman to remember when I was in Serbia."

"You mean hypnosis," Dr. Middlebach said. "That can help in certain circumstances, but results aren't guaranteed." He leaned a little closer. "Also, your friend has to be the one to ask for help. I can refer your friend to practicing psychologists. Many members of the faculty are also licensed to practice, and they sometimes will offer their time to someone who needs it." Dr. Middlebach sat back in his chair. "Does your friend feel sorry about what he's done?"

Luka nodded. "He thinks he is not good enough to be loved because of it."

Luka watched as deep-blue eyes scanned over him. Then Dr. Middlebach stood up and pulled a card from a holder on his desk. "Give this to your friend, and I'll see what I can do to help."

"Thank you," Luka said and extended his hand.

"Don't thank me yet. It might be very difficult for you to get your friend to ask for help. People who have been dealing with something this long tend to believe they can handle it and don't realize the benefits of talking to someone."

Luka smiled. "Thank you again. I will try."

Luka left the office, smiling at the lady sitting at her desk out front. He wished he could remember her name, but just said good-bye before hurrying back to the lab.

He spent the rest of the day immersed in his work. He tried not to think too much about Peter, but it was hard. He hadn't heard from him since Saturday and wondered if maybe he'd pushed too hard and Peter didn't want to see him anymore. Peter had told him all along that he didn't deserve anyone, so maybe this was his way of creating distance. More than once, Luka thought about calling, but stopped himself. He needed to wait until he was done with work. Then he would make the phone call.

Finally, after hours of tedious but necessary work categorizing and stringing together the genomes for a specific section of human DNA, Luka was exhausted and his eyes hurt. He said good night to Johnny and the others he worked with and left the building. He walked to the bus stop and waited for the bus that would begin his journey home.

Once he got on his feet, Luka intended to get a license and learn to drive here, but he didn't have the money and he figured there was no use going through the hassle of getting a license if he couldn't afford a car. Not that he minded, anyway. The bus wasn't so bad, and it gave him a chance to think.

The bus arrived and he got on, showed his pass, and then took a seat. Once they started to move, Luka pulled out his phone and dialed Peter's number.

"Hello, Peter," Luka said. "Do we have lesson tonight?"

"Um," Peter began, and Luka waited. "I guess we can. Where are you?"

"On the bus," Luka said. He'd been working on trying to use the little words he'd heard other people using. "I be home in...." He glanced at his watch. "Thirty minutes. I can cook for dinner."

Peter hesitated and then agreed. "I need to get my things first. I'll be there as soon as I can."

"Okay," Luka said with a smile. They disconnected, and he shoved the phone back in his pocket. He had to change buses and then walked the two blocks from the stop to his apartment. As he let himself in, the back door of the main house opened and Bella stepped out. She looked thin and tired, but it was good to see her out of the hospital. Luka forgot what he was doing, hurried over to her, and hugged her gently. "When you get home?"

"A few hours ago," she answered, and Luka helped her inside.

"You need rest," he said.

"I need to be around people. I'm tired of being alone. I have nothing to think about except Josif, and it's driving me crazy." Luka helped her up the few stairs and then through the house and into the living room. "My sister is supposed to come over anytime to visit." Bella sighed as she sat down. "All she's really coming for is to make sure I'm okay."

"Of course she is. She care about you. I care about you too."

"I know. And I want my sister to visit." She pulled a tissue from her sleeve. "I just want things to be the way they were."

Luka carefully pulled her into another hug. "I know." He thought about Misha and a lump formed in his throat. He didn't feel guilty for liking Peter, but that didn't dull the fact that sometimes he still missed his Misha very much. "It gets easier."

Bella nodded. "That's what everyone tells me." She'd taken the time to brush her dark hair, but the dark circles under her eyes hadn't dissipated completely, and she still seemed drawn and very sad. "I hope it's true."

"It is," Luka said.

Bella blew her nose and then sat back. "So, are you seeing Peter?"

"I don't know. I like him, but he's so sad too." That was the best word he could come up with.

"Peter has always been sad," Bella said. "He helps everyone, but never seems to get any true happiness for himself." She met Luka's eyes, and he held her gaze before turning away. But he wasn't fast enough. "You know why, don't you?"

Luka swallowed but didn't say a word.

"You do."

"Bella, I cannot…," he said.

"I won't ask you to betray what he told you," she said.

Luka heard noise from the back of the house.

"Are you expecting him?"

Luka nodded.

"Then go on. I won't be alone here for long. But please stop by whenever you want."

Luka promised he would and then walked back through the house. He met Peter at his door, and they went inside.

Neither of them said anything as Peter spread his books on the table.

"Do you hate me?" Luka finally asked.

"No. Why would I hate you?"

"You no talk to me," Luka said.

"I don't know what to say," Peter said and then slid into one of the chairs. "I like you. I do. And it scares me."

"Why?"

"Because I'm not supposed to be happy. I don't deserve it," Peter told him. "When I'm with you I forget sometimes about… what happened." He shifted in the chair until their gazes met. "What if I hurt you?"

"I no understand," Luka said, approaching Peter slowly. "It was accident, and it time you forgive you. Mama and Vince and

Julie do not matter. *You* need to forgive you. That where it starts."
He knew that in his heart.

"I can't," Peter said. "Don't you think I've tried?"

Luka sighed. He thought Peter had tried, but maybe he hadn't
done it the right way. "Do not hate me," Luka whispered. He
reached into his pocket and placed Dr. Middlebach's card in Peter's
hand.

"Why would I...." Peter shifted his gaze to the card, and Luka
saw his expression darken, like a storm cloud forming on a sunny
day. "What is this?"

"He the head of the psychology department." He stumbled
slightly over the words in his nervousness. "I see him today, and he
say that he will try to help."

"You told him?" Peter bellowed.

Luka's instinct was to take a step back, but he forced his feet
still. "No. I tell him I have friend who need help. He say he will try.
But you must be one to ask." Luka shook slightly. "You call or no
call, it up to you." He shrugged, trying to seem casual.

"Why would you do this?" Peter asked, his expression hard.

"You help all the time. No shame in asking for help for you,"
Luka said, forcing himself to use English, because if he switched to
Serbian he'd only yell and that wouldn't do anyone any good.
"Please see him. Maybe he help you."

Peter's expression softened, but he still looked hurt. Luka had
known he was taking a chance in approaching this subject at all. He
still expected Peter to leave, and if he did, Luka wondered if he'd
ever come back.

"I don't need this kind of help," Peter said, handing Luka back
the card.

"You want what happened to change. It can't. You need to talk
about it. He can help." Luka scratched his head, wondering if there
was anything he could say to convince Peter. He handed the card
back to Peter. "You keep. Think on it." Luka moved to the table and
sat down. He thought it was best to change the subject and not push.
Looking over at Peter, he waited, hoping they could get to work.

Luka noticed Peter shoved the card in his pocket. For all he knew it would simply end up going through the laundry. But he hoped Peter would use it. They got to work and spent the next hour on intensive speech and what Peter called "vocabulary." By the time they were done, Luka's head was swimming. Peter left him some exercises to do and then began gathering his things.

"You do not have to leave," Luka said, using some of the new phrasing he'd learned.

Peter smiled. "That was very good. But I need to go."

Luka reached out for his hand. "I do not want to make you feel bad," he said. "I want to help like you help me."

"It's not the same," Peter said.

Luka chuckled nervously. "It not the same because you not the one helping." He folded his arms over his chest waiting, for Peter to say he was wrong. Peter started back at him intently, and Luka returned his gaze. He wasn't going to back down. Luka felt he was right. "Let you be helped," he said. Peter looked away. Luka tightened his hold on his hand in case he decided to run.

"I won't make any promises." Peter's stance softened, and Luka guided him away from the kitchen table to the sofa. They sat down, and Luka moved closer. He'd missed Peter.

A brisk knock sounded on his door. At first he thought about ignoring it, but it came again, and Luka worried it was Bella. He got up and turned to take a quick look at Peter before walking to the door. He opened it.

"*Zdravo*, Luka," said a man he'd never seen before.

"Who are you?" Luka responded in Serbian and glanced over to where Peter sat. He saw him lean forward as Luka turned back to the man.

"A friend from your home," he answered in a rather menacing tone that put Luka instantly on edge.

"This is my home how," he clarified. "Please leave." Luka heard Peter get up and walk toward him. Luka didn't dare take his eyes off the stranger. He sensed Peter's approach and felt him come up behind him. "I live here and do not intend to return."

"But you did not have permission to leave," the man said.

"He's here legally," Peter said in perfect Serbian from behind him. The man's eyes widened. "Who are you?"

"I'm Dragomir Nicolic with the Serbian diplomatic mission," the man said in careful English. "We only want him to know that his friends and family at home miss him." His gaze never left Luka. "We only want to be sure Luka is adjusting to life here." He smiled the toothy grin of a tiger who'd just spotted its prey.

"Luka is just fine," Peter said, and Luka felt warmth on his back, like Peter was just about to touch him.

Dragomir handed him a card. Luka took it and closed the door. He watched out the side window to make sure the man left and then slumped back. He should have known the peace and quiet were too good to be true.

"They know where you live," Peter said.

Luka nodded. "They were also giving me a warning," he began in Serbian. "I still have family and a few friends in Serbia. They were telling me I better keep quiet about certain parts of my work in Serbia or they could make trouble for them." Luka's hand shook as he set the card on the table, not wanting to hold it any longer.

"Will they try to hurt you?" Peter asked, wrapping his arms around Luka's waist.

"I don't know," Luka answered, thankful Peter hadn't switched back to English. "I should have known something like this would happen. I was working on secret programs." He took a deep breath. "I hope they will leave me alone now that they have delivered their message."

"He came quite a ways to deliver a message. I think the nearest consulate is in Chicago," Peter said.

That didn't surprise Luka. Not that he was that important, but they had to let him know he was being watched. "They will lose interest in me after a few months. I would never betray their confidence, just like I would not betray secrets I learn in my work here." He tried to calm his rapidly beating heart. "If they wanted to hurt me or to do more than talk, they would not have announced themselves."

He felt Peter nod and tighten the hold around his waist. "I don't want you to be alone," Peter whispered into his ear.

The Serbian words in Peter's soft voice sent a ripple through him. "Then you stay. I cook," Luka said in English, but Peter shook his head. Luka's heart plummeted to the floor.

"I can't. I haven't been home yet and I need to take care of Milton. You can come with me, though."

Luka smiled and nodded. "Let me got some clothes and then I need to let Bella know I'm going to be gone. She just got home." He turned in time to see Peter smile. "She would be happy to see you." Peter nodded, and Luka slipped away and up the stairs to his small, sparse sleeping area. He got his small bag and packed it with a change of clothes and the things he'd need to clean up and shave. The last thing he did was glance at the photographs of his parents and Misha, the only adornment in the room and nearly all he'd been able to bring from his former life.

Then Luka descended the stairs. Peter was waiting for him, and they left together, locked the door, and walked through the yard to the main house.

Bella was pleased to see them. She introduced them to her sister, Sima, and they talked for a few minutes. Luka told her he was going to be gone and saw the pleased little smile she gave him. He didn't tell her about Dragomir's visit, and they left before she got too tired out.

"How did Dragomir know where to find you?" Peter asked as they wove through traffic. "It's not as if you've advertised where you live."

"I have felt like I've been watched sometimes," Luka said. "I've seen people in the alley." It didn't mean they were watching him, though. At home, he'd often known someone was watching. He hated that feeling and had come here, in part, to try to escape it.

"I suppose there are ways of finding anyone if you want to badly enough," Peter said.

Luka nodded and looked out the window, checking to see if they were being followed. He knew that was probably a stupid notion, because if they were being followed, he probably wouldn't see them. But he still watched. He saw nothing, of course, but he couldn't help it. He also wondered if he should have told Bella everything, but he didn't want to worry her. Luka hoped that if he was away from her, she would be safer

They arrived at Peter's and went inside. Milton pranced and rubbed around both their legs before running off toward the kitchen. Peter followed, and Luka went along with him. After feeding the cat, Peter began making dinner. Luka helped where he could, and they sat down to a dinner of pasta and salad. Luka had noticed that Americans tended to underseason their food for his taste. The food he'd grown up with was vibrantly spiced, sometimes hot, but always bursting with flavor. Not that what Peter had made wasn't good, but…. Luka figured he was probably getting a little homesick. Maybe next time he would cook. They talked as they ate, but once again, it felt more like a language exercise than a real conversation. It seemed like there was something else in the room with them. Luka was afraid it was the conversation about the psychologist, but it could just as easily be the people from the Serbian government watching him. Or maybe Peter was simply getting tired of him.

When they were done eating, Peter cleared the dishes. Luka offered to help, but Peter declined and went to clean up. "You can watch television if you want. This won't take long."

"Okay," Luka said. He stood up and stepped into the living room. He sat on the sofa, and Milton jumped up and walked back and forth on his lap a few times before jumping back to the floor. Luka didn't turn on the television. The shows were too loud, and he rarely found anything interesting. He waited for Peter to finish in the kitchen and then sit down next to him.

"Do you really think I need help?" Peter asked, pulling the card from his pocket.

"It not hurt," Luka said. He let himself hope a little more that Peter would contact Dr. Middlebach, but he didn't want to press.

"In my job I've referred many people to counseling. I suppose I should take my own advice," Peter said eventually and then turned toward him, smiling. Luka moved closer as the distance that had settled between them lifted like a fog. "I mean, you cared enough to speak with him."

"I did not ask to hurt you. I want to help," Luka said, much relieved.

Peter shifted closer as well. Their lips met, and Luka moaned softly. The kiss deepened, and Luka wrapped his arms around Peter's neck, tugging him down on top of him. Peter's shoes hit the carpet with muffled thumps, and Luka's quickly followed. Shirts and pants joined the pile until Luka and Peter were pressed together, skin to skin. Luka quickly lost himself in taste and touch. Very few things in life could compare to one of Peter's kisses, let alone the way his skin felt against Luka's.

"Shall we go to the bedroom?" Peter whispered, slowly climbing off him and the sofa. Then he tugged Luka to his feet and held his hand as they walked to the bedroom.

Luka felt a little ridiculous as he walked into Peter's bedroom in nothing but his socks. But the thought slipped from his mind when Peter closed the door behind them, gathered Luka into his arms, and kissed him hard enough that Luka expected his knees to buckle.

"I should never have gotten angry with you," Peter said when he broke their kiss. "You were only thinking of me, and maybe your friend can help me feel better. I don't know if it's possible, but I'll try."

"Oh," Luka responded and smiled wide, wriggling his hips slightly, and Peter gasped quietly. Now that was the best kind of communication Luka could think of. Sometimes words were overrated. "No talk now," Luka whispered into Peter's ear before sucking on it lightly. Peter moaned again, and Luka sucked harder.

Within seconds Peter had Luka turned around and pressed back against the bed and then down onto the mattress. Peter chuckled, and Luka went right along with him. He was happy, and Peter sounded happy as well. Luka stretched and wrapped his lips around one of Peter's nipples, sucking slightly. Peter's chuckles shifted to a deep, throaty moan. "I love that sound," Luka said, licking Peter's skin and then blowing on it. Peter quivered, and Luka did it again. "You need touch," Luka told him.

"I need what?"

Rather than explain, Luka stretched like a cat, touching Peter in as many places as possible, running his hands over his chest and down his side. "To be touched," he said.

"I don't know what you mean. Maybe you should show me again."

Peter was playing, and Luka grinned up at him. Peter was very serious all the time. To hear him being playful was a surprise. Luka hadn't thought Peter could be like that. But he was now. Luka stroked him again, lightening his touch as he went down Peter's side. Peter squirmed and giggled like a girl when Luka tickled him.

"That wasn't nice."

"You laugh like girl," Luka teased.

Peter's expression calmed, his eyes widening. Then before Luka could react, Peter rolled them on the bed, pressing Luka into the mattress.

Luka laughed when Peter tickled him in return. He tried to get away, but Peter held him close. It took a few seconds for the sensation to die before he realized that Peter was no longer tickling him. Instead, he was licking and sucking his way along Luka's chest. "That nice," Luka whispered. "I think I keep you."

"You do, huh?" Peter challenged. "What if I want to keep you?"

"Then we keep each other," Luka countered. He wasn't sure exactly what they'd just said to each other, but it seemed momentous a few seconds after he said the words. Luka waited for Peter's reaction. There had to be one.

Their eyes met, and Peter opened his mouth. Luka slid an arm around Peter's neck, drew him close, and kissed him. Whatever Peter was about to say, Luka could wait to hear it. If Peter was going to argue or make excuses, now was not the time or place to hear it. When Peter moaned again, Luka knew he'd at least put off his inevitable arguments. That was fine for now. He didn't want to hear them right after what he'd just said.

Peter rubbed against him, slowly moving up and down, sliding their cocks along each other. That was nice. No, way more than nice.

Luka shifted and tried to move. Peter lifted himself up and settled beside him. Luka rolled onto his belly and spread his legs wide, issuing Peter an invitation.

"You're beautiful," Peter whispered and kissed his shoulder.

Luka groaned softly as Peter slid up his back, slowly pressing his solid weight down on him. He'd always loved this position. With Misha, and now Peter, it made him feel safe, surrounded by someone he cared for. Peter licked and kissed his shoulder and then down his back. Luka arched his back slightly into the hot wetness, holding his breath to see what Peter would do. When Peter settled hot hands on his butt, followed by his lips and tongue doing magic things to his skin, Luka stretched, pressing his hands to the headboard. "Peter," rumbled from deep in his throat. He held his breath as Peter kneaded his cheeks and licked his skin, coming closer and closer to his opening. Luka closed his eyes, praying for Peter to go farther.

He did. Luka whined softly, on the verge of begging. He ended up uttering a steady stream of endearments and mild curses in Serbian when Peter licked and probed him with his hot, wet tongue.

After rimming him to within an inch of his life, Peter pulled away. Luka was breathless and already well on his way to nirvana. He shivered with anticipation as he heard the drawer next to the bed open, then the familiar sound of a condom wrapper being torn open and the squelch of a bottle.

"Is this okay?" Peter whispered.

Luka lifted his backside to let Peter know he was more than ready. Peter spread his legs wider, settled between them, and then pressed to Luka's opening. Luka held his breath and forced his muscles to relax. Peter was not small, by any stretch, and when he pushed forward, Luka groaned long and loud as Peter breached him.

Peter stopped just inside. Luka hissed his breath through his teeth, eyes rolling as the burn washed over him, morphing quickly to extreme pleasure. Peter must have sensed that exact moment, because he pressed forward, filling Luka to the brim. Luka gave up trying to talk and listened to Peter.

He arched his back, pressing his butt upward, buried his face in one of the pillows, and rode the waves of ecstasy. Peter started slow and then began moving faster. He didn't go too fast, though, and within minutes Luka hung onto the edge, expecting to plunge over at any second. Peter had other ideas and held him there, teetering on the edge, before wrapping his arms around him.

"Come for me, sweetheart," Peter whispered into his ear, and Luka plummeted into his release.

Luka gasped and then stilled. Peter rested on top of him, holding him tight. Then, slowly, Luka shifted. He groaned softly as their bodies disconnected. Peter settled on the bed next to him, and Luka closed his eyes, letting the warmth wash over him. He heard and felt Peter move. He got up, and Luka watched Peter as he left the room and then returned a minute later. Peter smiled at him and climbed back into bed, hugging him tight.

"What changed your mind?" Luka asked. "About the psychology," he clarified. He figured he was using the term incorrectly, but he didn't know the correct one.

"You did. When I saw that Dragomir guy at your door, I realized...." Peter swallowed. "I realized I have feelings for you and I care about you."

Luka rolled over to face Peter. There was a lot in Peter's voice that he wasn't saying. Luka wished he knew what it was and how to read it. Instead, all he could do was listen carefully to Peter's words.

"If I felt that way about you, then I thought you might feel the same way about me and would want to help."

"I do want to help," Luka said.

Peter's expression shifted, his features harder. "I'm not convinced it will do any good. But since I've never tried, I don't know. I'm willing to give it a try, though." He sighed. "I'll call him in the morning and see what he says."

Luka smiled and nodded. Then he angled closer for a kiss. He wound his arms around Peter's neck and deepened the kiss, holding him close. "You help me, I help you," Luka said, and Peter nodded.

There were so many things he didn't know. Luka kept hoping some of Peter's walls were breaking down and he was opening himself up to being happy. But he wasn't sure. He didn't need to speak English to know that ideas held for a long time didn't change overnight. Peter had felt he wasn't worthy of love or even kindness for such a long time, and Luka knew it wouldn't change quickly. He needed to be patient. Finding someone to speak with who would help him and reinforce that what had happened when he was six did not make him a bad person and didn't mean he shouldn't be loved might go a long way to letting Peter find some happiness. Luka hoped that when Peter opened his heart, it was to him, because his own heart had already opened and allowed Peter inside.

"What are you thinking about?" Peter asked. "You look so serious."

Luka closed his eyes. He wondered if he should say anything, but figured telling Peter how he felt would only make Peter retreat to his usual arguments, so he kept quiet. "Nothing," he whispered. Peter turned out the lights, and Luka closed his eyes.

Pawing sounds at the door made Luka chuckle, and he got up and let Milton in the room. The cat scolded him as he walked across the room and jumped onto the bed. Luka joined Peter back in bed, closing his eyes. How long he lay listening to Peter's soft breathing and Milton's purrs, he didn't know.

Chapter 7

PETER LEFT the office of Dr. Middlebach, still surprised the highly placed academic would work with him directly. It had taken Peter nearly a full day to actually make the call. He'd been pleased at how personable and easy Franz was to talk with. He'd almost immediately requested that they use first names as well as spent the first part of their time together asking questions that Peter was certain were designed to make him comfortable and get him to open up.

Peter had been reluctant at first to tell Franz what had happened when he was a child, but eventually he realized he had to open up, so he told Franz the same story he'd told Luka. A few times he'd seen Franz show surprise, but he never detected any judgment. Once he'd finished telling Dr. Middlebach the story of his father's death, Peter continued. The floodgates seemed to have opened, and he explained how he'd always felt about his family.

"I'm puzzled," Franz began once Peter had finished. "Usually people feel guilty or ashamed of things but don't know why, or they hide it. And once the source of the guilt and shame is out in the open, it loses some of its power. Yours, however, has been reinforced over decades. There was never any way for you to escape it, and it became ingrained as part of who you are and part of your personality."

"Is there any way you can help?" Peter asked.

"I think so. I'd like to meet again if you're agreeable," Franz said.

Peter had nodded and shifted his gaze to the floor. "I need to know how much this is going to cost."

"Nothing," Franz said. "I'd only like your permission to use my findings in my research. I will not use your actual name to protect your privacy."

Peter had initially been reluctant, but if his situation could help someone else.... He had eventually agreed, and he and Franz set up a series of appointments for the coming weeks. He felt better. He didn't know why, other than talking to someone who hadn't judged him once he'd heard what Peter had done. He took a deep breath and released it, walking taller and feeling just a little bit lighter.

Over the next week, he saw Franz twice more. Their sessions focused somewhat on Peter shooting his father, but they also began to range further afield, with Peter talking in depth about his family and, of course, about Luka.

"You smile when you speak of him," Franz observed. "Did you know you do that each time?"

"Is that bad?" Peter asked seriously.

"Quite the opposite," Franz said. "But I'd like to explore why you would think it's bad... or could be bad." He reached for a notepad. "Why would someone making you happy be bad? You obviously care for him."

Peter sighed. "I killed one of the people in the world who loved me most. I guess I've never thought I deserved to have someone in my life like Luka." He paused for a few seconds. "Luka says I do a lot of the things I do because I'm trying to make up for what I did to my dad."

Franz nodded slowly. "You just smiled slightly as you mentioned his name."

"Oh," Peter said.

"You shouldn't be ashamed of those feelings. They're good and show you getting on with your life. What you did at six should not define you for the rest of your life. And it won't as long as you don't let it." Franz consulted his notes, and Peter waited. "I'd like to try a few things if we can."

Peter nodded and sat back in the chair. "What did you have in mind?"

"I'd like you to describe your brother to me. Tell me what he's like. What are his good personality traits and what about him annoys you?"

"Well, Vince is two years older than me, and he has twin girls. He's a great father and loves those two girls to death."

"What was he like growing up?" Franz asked, continuing to make notes.

"Like most of other kids, I guess," Peter answered, scratching the back of his neck.

"Did he pick on you or go out of his way to make you feel guilty?" Franz asked.

Peter thought for a few seconds. "Not really. My sister and mother were more vocal in that regard, I guess. Vince always seemed quiet. He's very smart, but has always been quiet."

"What sort of things did your mother and sister do?" Franz asked.

"My mother never said anything about shooting my father, but she always made me guilty whenever she wanted something. She still does, and I think Julie picked that up from her. I knew I didn't have a leg to stand on because it was my fault that Dad was gone, so I guess I always tried to do what they wanted so they would like me and possibly forgive me." Peter blew his breath from his lungs. "Of course, there was nothing I could ever do. And I suppose the more I tried to make up for what I'd done, the more they took advantage of it. I was always grateful to Vince that he never acted that way." Peter swallowed.

"You speak as though you think he's a good guy."

Peter shrugged. "I think he is, I guess. Are you trying to get at something?"

"Not necessarily. I was just curious how you saw the people you grew up with. What does your sister do well?"

"You mean besides guilt?" Peter quipped and chuckled softly. "Julie is a younger version of my mother."

"But Vince is different," Franz said. "Why do you think that is?"

Peter paused. "I never gave it much thought. Maybe because he's a guy."

Franz said nothing, and the silence began making Peter uncomfortable.

"It could be because he was there and feels partially at fault. But he wasn't the one who pulled the trigger."

"No," Franz said. "But he was the one who found the gun and was playing with it. Did you and Vince ever talk about what happened that day?"

"A few times, but he never really wanted to talk about it and would always change the subject. Not that I wanted to talk about it much." Peter looked around the office, his gaze settling on a small statue of a horse sitting on one of the bookshelves. "As a kid I used to hope that if I never brought it up, they might start to forget. Of course that was dumb, but I was a kid."

"What did Vince say when you talked to him?"

Peter closed his eyes and tried to remember. They hadn't talked about that day in years. "I guess he said once that he was sorry he'd ever found the gun."

"But nothing about you shooting your dad?" Franz asked. "I mean, did he ever actually say you did it?"

"What are you getting at?" Peter asked, snapping his head around.

"Nothing. I'm only asking questions," Franz said. A small timer went off, and Peter exhaled. "I'd like to try something for our next visit. See if Luka will be willing to come to the appointment."

"Sort of a group session?"

"No. We're going to try a few exercises, and if you're okay with it, I'd like there to be someone with you whom you trust. It's up to you, of course."

Peter nodded. "That would be fine. He knows I'm speaking with you, and he's remarked on the difference in me."

"And what difference is that?" Franz asked.

Peter hesitated. "The best I can describe, it feels like I can breathe freely. Like I'm not always walking on eggshells."

"Then if nothing else comes out of this, you've been helped."

Peter nodded. "Most definitely." He stood up, and as he always did, shook Franz's hand and got ready to leave.

"Please think about our next session."

"I will," Peter agreed and walked toward the door. "Thank you for doing this."

Franz smiled at him. "You're most welcome." He stood as well. "This has been good for me as well. I got into psychology to help people, but these days I spend most of my time pushing papers." He opened the office door. "Take care, and I'll see you on Thursday."

Peter left the office and then the building, heading to the parking lot. He got into his car and drove back to work. He'd just reached the building and was pulling into the only parking spot available in the lot when his phone rang. Peter finished parking and placed the car in park before seeing who it was. He groaned when he saw the number.

"Hi, Mom," he said when he answered it.

"I'm going blind," she told him.

Peter stilled completely and waited for more. His mother could be dramatic.

"Okay… what exactly did the doctor say?" Peter asked cautiously. "What exactly was the diagnosis?" His mind shifted to programs he could send his mother to that would help her adjust to her new sight-challenged state.

"He said I'm developing cataracts and should no longer be driving. That's why I need rides everywhere. They want to schedule surgery." He could hear the fear in his mother's voice. She had had appendicitis a few years ago and had nearly died because she kept insisting she was going to be fine and would not let anyone "cut into her."

"Cataracts are easily treated, Mom. I think they do one eye and then the other," he explained. "It's no big deal, and once it's done, you'll be able to see like you did years ago, and then you'll be able to drive again." He was trying to be reasonable.

"That's easy for you to say. You're not the one whose eyes they want to cut into," she snapped. "Someone will have to stay with me while I'm recovering, and I can't ask Julie because she's busy, and Vince has the kids...."

"Mother, Julie lives with you. Of course she can help take care of you."

"Well...," she began. "I hate to ask her. So I thought you could come stay with me for a few weeks."

Peter took a deep breath. He hated it when his mother and sister asked him for things like this. He knew his mother just wanted him around to fetch and carry for her, as well as listen to her complain about everything, including him.

"No, Mother," he finally said. "I can't move in with you for a few weeks. I have work, classes, and appointments. Traveling in from Mequon through rush-hour traffic every day isn't practical when my clients are in the heart of the city."

"I need your help and you're telling me no?" she asked. "You, of all people...."

"That's enough of that, Mom. I can't do it, and Julie most certainly can. I can help take you places if you need, but you'll have to make arrangements in advance," Peter said, and some of the pain he'd been carrying slipped away. *Some.* He still felt guilty for telling her no, but he pushed it aside as best he could. She wasn't being reasonable, and Peter had no doubt his sister would try calling as well. "I love you, Mom, but I'm not going to be your guilt-filled pushover any longer." He smiled as he got out of the car, locked it, and headed inside his building. "I really hope you have the procedure. It will help you see and give you back some of the independence you've lost. Let me know when you're having it done and I'll be there to support you. But Julie needs to help as well. Now, if she wants to get her own place, then maybe...."

Peter could hear his mother inhale, getting ready to argue. It was what she always did. Why he'd never seen it before, he didn't know, but he knew exactly what he was going to do: he wasn't going to allow it. "I have to go in to work. Think about what the doctor said. I know people who have been through the same thing and I'm sure they'll talk to you to help put your mind at ease." He walked toward the building and pulled the door open, then walked through the lobby to the elevator. "I'll talk to you soon," he said gently and then hung up. He sighed as he put his phone in his pocket.

By the time he got to his desk, he'd already started doubting his decision and all the things he'd said to his mother, but it was too late to take them back.

WORK KEPT him hopping for the rest of the day. By the time he was done, he was exhausted and still worried about the conversation with his mother. Luka expected him for dinner, and usually that was the highlight of his day, but he was worried about asking him to his next therapy session. He wasn't sure why he was so nervous. He knew he was being ridiculous about it.

Peter stopped at home after work, gave Milton some attention and fed him before heading out to Luka's. He parked in the usual place, went to the door, and knocked softly. He didn't get an answer and looked toward the main house, wondering if Luka was there. He was about to knock when he heard soft whistling. When he stepped out into the alley, he saw Luka coming toward him.

"What has you so happy?" Peter asked with a smile.

"You're here, and I had... a...." Luka paused. "Breakthrough," he said in Serbian. "It was very good."

"I'm glad." Peter grinned. He loved seeing Luka happy. "You haven't seen any more of the guy from Serbia, have you?" he asked while Luka opened the door.

"Once, a few days ago. I was ready to call the police like you said," Luka explained as he opened the door. "But he cannot do anything to me here."

Peter knew that wasn't exactly true, but he didn't want to dampen Luka's happiness and wished he hadn't said anything.

"Did you have your appointment with Dr. Middlebach?" Luka placed his bag on the seat of one of the chairs and turned toward him expectantly.

Peter nodded and shifted his weight from foot to foot. "We had a good talk today. I'm not sure what I told him that he found so interesting, but he said he wants to do something different at our next appointment, and he asked if I'd like to have you come with me. He said that whatever he wants to do works better when someone I trust is there." Peter shifted slightly. "Will you come?"

Luka smiled. "Of course. When is appointment?"

"Thursday at four," Peter answered.

Luka nodded and stepped closer, tilting his head slightly. A knock on the door made them both jump. Luka kissed him quickly and then turned. He peered out of the window and then opened it. Bella stepped inside. Her hair had been done, but she still had the look of someone who hadn't been sleeping very well. Peter pulled out the other kitchen chair and motioned her into it. She wobbled a bit and sat down.

"What is wrong?" Luka asked. He scurried to get her a glass of water and placed it on the table in front of her.

"Nothing," Bella said. "There's nothing to live for. I sit in that house with nothing to do and either wait for people to visit me or wish Josif was still here." She sipped from the glass and put it back down. "I don't want to be a burden to anyone, but I saw your car and…." Bella stood up. "I should have left you alone."

"Sit down," Peter said, and she lowered herself in the chair again. "You don't have to go anywhere. I just got here." Peter looked at Luka. "When I saw you coming through the yard, I thought you'd been at Bella's."

"I get home from work. Came through the yard," Luka explained. "Bella, you stay for dinner," he added, turning to her.

Peter nodded his agreement.

"I'm cooking cevaps."

Peter saw him swallow hard, sadness appearing on his face for a few seconds.

"They were Misha's favorite." Luka smiled slightly. He stepped closer and gave Peter a kiss, then turned and opened the small refrigerator, pulled out the meat, and went to the cupboard for the other ingredients.

Bella fidgeted on her chair. "Is there something you want to talk about?" Peter asked, sitting down across from Bella. He knew enough to stay out of the way. It was a small kitchen, and Luka knew what he was doing.

"When I went to the doctor last week, he ran some more tests, and I got a call this afternoon," Bella explained. Her hands shook. The room turned silent, both he and Luka stilling. "The doctor said I'm pregnant." Bella got the words out and then burst into tears.

The sharp ring of metal slapping the counter filled the room, and then Luka was next to Bella, putting his arms around her. "That's wonderful," he said in Serbian. "The child will be blessed."

Bella continued crying. "The doctor says that because of the accident, the child might not be right. He says I must have gotten pregnant just a few days before the accident. He said that while I was unconscious, there might have been damage to the child, and that I shouldn't get my hopes up."

Luka released Bella and swore under his breath. Then he swore louder, filling the room with Serbian curses that would make the roughest construction worker blush. "They not know nothing," Luka said. "This is Serbian baby, he be strong and full of life." Luka released Bella and turned, rummaging in one of the cupboards until he found a bottle. He then got two glasses and poured a small amount into each. Luka placed a glass in front of Peter and lifted his own in the air. "To Josif and to the baby," he said in rapid Serbian before downing the shot in a single gulp. Peter did the same, and nearly coughed as the liquor burned down his throat. "I give you some, but it is bad for the baby," Luka told Bella, who smiled. "This is good news. Doctor not know Serbian babies. Strong." He made a muscle, and Peter chuckled.

Luka went back to cooking.

"The baby will be healthy," Peter said. "You got good care while you were in the hospital, and I'm sure the doctor will schedule a lot of checkups and tests to check on the baby."

"I know, but what if he's right?" Bella asked.

"Doctors today are all about helping you make choices. They don't have all the answers. The baby was very small when you were injured." Peter took a deep breath. "Think of it this way—right now, you have a small piece of Josif with you. It's growing by the minute, and in eight months, you'll have Josif's child. There's nothing more wonderful than that." He glanced at Luka as he worked the ground meat and spices in a bowl, filling the room with the scents of paprika, onion, and garlic. "This is truly good news."

"I want it to be," Bella said. "But I'm afraid."

"Why are you scared?" Luka asked, the bowl dinging on the counter.

"Raising a child alone...," Bella said.

Luka stopped what he was doing and stepped closer, his hands covered with the meat and spices. "You are not alone. I am here, Peter is here, your family is here. Everyone helps and loves this baby. There is nothing to be scared for. I love the baby already," Luka said, meeting Bella's gaze.

Peter turned away as tears formed in his eyes. He swallowed hard as he realized just how lucky he was. Somehow, of all the people in the world, he'd managed to meet and catch the eye of one of the most loving people he could ever know. He blinked a few times as he wondered why he'd never seen it before.

"Thank you," Bella said.

Peter moved closer to Bella and took her hand. "You're going to be an amazing mother. And Luka's right. You don't have to do this alone. There are a lot of people in your life who will be willing to help. I love children." He thought about Vince's twins and sniffed. He'd been largely cut out of their lives. He wasn't sure how it had happened, but.... "And I'd be honored to have a place in your child's life."

Bella began to cry again.

Luka looked at him, and Peter tried to comfort her while Luka went back to cooking. "There's no reason to cry. Everything is going to be great,"

"But what if there's something... wrong with the baby?" She started weeping again.

Peter found a tissue and handed it to her.

"Your baby is going to be as strong as you are." Peter looked over at Luka, who had begun forming the sausages. "So you need to eat and take care of yourself, because you're also taking care of that baby." Peter paused. "Look, I've seen healthy children born to drug addicts and people who smoked two packs of cigarettes a day. This early in the pregnancy, all anyone can say is that your baby is at greater risk than others because of what happened. That's all. Did the doctor give you any instructions?"

"He said to start taking prenatal vitamins and to eat well. The usual stuff. Don't drink and stay away from cigarette smoke."

"See? He hasn't given up hope, so you shouldn't either," Peter told her with a smile.

Bella dried her eyes and sniffed a few times. "Thank you," she whispered.

"There's nothing to thank me for. I'm so happy for you I could burst," Peter told her. "I like to think that we have to take the good with the bad. We all make mistakes and somehow we right the karmic balance. You lost Josif, and this is the universe's way of rebalancing the scale."

Bella nodded slowly. "Maybe you're right." She sniffed a few times and wiped her nose. Then she stood up and threw the tissue away before washing her hands. "What can I do to help? I've been sitting around for days and I need something to make myself useful."

"There is lettuce in the refrigerator. You may make salad," Luka said.

"Your English is getting better," Bella said.

"I try. Peter has been helping me, but it is hard and everyone says it takes time," Luka explained. "I really want to speak good."

"Speak well," Peter corrected. "And I wish all the people I work with learned and progressed as quickly as you have."

"Am I interrupting the lessons?" Bella asked as she tore the lettuce into a bowl.

"No. We were just spending some time together this evening." Lately Peter had been trying to regiment the language work they did together. He and Luka had been spending so much time together he was afraid they'd let the lessons fall by the wayside, and he didn't want that. The sooner Luka grasped English, the better off he would be, both at work and in his personal life. "We'll work together tomorrow evening for an hour or so."

"I always working to learn," Luka said. "I listen to television and watch videos so I can speak better." Luka finished with the sausages and began heating up a pan. Peter cleared and set the table, then brought in one of the small chairs from the other room. With the three of them, the table would be cozy, but that was probably what Bella needed.

Once dinner was ready, they all sat down at the table. Luka poured drinks, and they toasted to Bella's happiness and the health of the baby with water—plain, pure water. Then they all began to eat. The meal was fairly quiet. Bella seemed lost in her own thoughts. Peter kept catching Luka's eye, and a few times Bella caught them.

"You two. Go ahead and make doe eyes at each other," she said when she caught Peter looking away. "You should be happy together."

After eating, Luka took care of the dishes. Bella excused herself and said good night, accepting hugs from both of them before leaving.

"She ate well," Luka commented as he watched her leave. "There are going to be hard times for her."

"Yes, but there will be happy times again for her as well," Peter whispered and followed Luka back inside once Bella's door closed. "Just like there will be for me."

Luka turned around and wrapped his arms around Peter's waist. "I always knew there would be."

"I didn't. I never thought I could ever possibly deserve them. Hell, I'm still not sure that I do. But Franz keeps telling me the same thing you do." Peter paused and leaned in for a kiss. "You know what he said to me today?"

Luka shook his head.

"He said that when I talk about you, I smile. I never realized I did that, but I do." Peter couldn't help smiling right that second. "You make me happy, Luka. You're kind, thoughtful, caring, and strong all at the same time." He closed his eyes. "It's hard for me to say this because I'm not really sure I know what the words mean, but I love you, Luka." Peter took a deep breath. "I know I don't deserve it, but I love you anyway. Maybe that's selfish or wishful thinking, but I hope you can...."

"Volim te," Luka said quietly, and Peter felt tears build in his eyes. He'd longed to hear someone say they loved him. And he knew the words came from Luka's heart. Peter cupped Luka's cheeks in his hands and brought their lips together.

"I want to show you how I feel, not just tell you," Peter whispered.

Luka nodded and pulled Peter into a tight embrace.

Luka turned out the lights as they made their way through the room and up the stairs. Neither spoke. Peter's heart pounded in his ears as they approached the bed. He was nervous and felt like he had years ago, when he was about to lose his virginity.

"What is wrong?" Luka asked. Normally Peter would have commented on the addition of the verb Luka sometimes still left out, but he was too keyed up and barely noticed. "You are shaking."

Peter nodded. "It's hard to explain." He sat on the edge of the bed. "I've done this before. We've done this before." Peter motioned toward the bed. "But it seems different this time."

"Of course is different," Luka said, moving closer, until he stood between Peter's legs. "This making love, not just... fucking? Is that right word?"

"Sex is probably a better one, but I get your meaning," Peter said.

"This is your first time... making love," Luka said. "That why you nervous. I nervous too." Luka took his hand and placed it over his rapidly beating heart. "That because of you." He then placed his hand over Peter's chest. "I feel you too." Luka locked his gaze onto Peter's.

Peter's excitement soared to the roof. He shifted slightly for comfort, but nothing seemed to help. He was as excited as he could ever remember being, but scared at the same time.

"What if I mess this up?" Peter asked. He didn't expect an answer, because there really wasn't one, and he felt a bit dumb for saying the question out loud.

"Follow what is here," Luka said, patting his chest. Then he moved closer and covered Peter's lips with his.

Fire shot through Peter, and he gasped and then moaned loudly.

Luka pressed him back, and Peter went willingly.

"Let me love you," Luka said.

Peter nodded his assent.

Luka slowly, deliberately, and sensually removed Peter's clothes, kissing and licking the exposed skin. He seemed intent on taking his time. Once Peter was finally divested of the last of his clothing, his entire body throbbed and he couldn't see straight. Luka was still completely dressed, staring down at him. In the past, a situation like this would have left him feeling vulnerable, but with Luka it was incredibly naughty and sexy feeling. And the way Luka looked at him took Peter's breath away.

"You are handsome," Luka whispered, kneeling on the bed next to him, slowly rubbing his chest and belly.

Whenever Luka sent his hands south, Peter stilled, praying Luka would touch him, but he only skimmed around his throbbing cock without touching it. More than once Peter thought he would scream, but instead gripped the bedding tighter and whimpered.

Finally, Luka unbuttoned his shirt, shrugged it off his shoulders, and dropped it behind him. Peter sat up to reach for him, but Luka pressed him back against the mattress with the gentlest touch. Luka's gaze burned into him so hot and deep that the thump of Luka's shoes falling to the floor barely registered. Then Luka stepped off the bed. He turned around and slipped his pants down his legs, giving Peter a stellar view of his perfect bubble backside. He reached out to touch, but Luka moved out of reach. Peter sighed and settled back on the bed.

When Luka turned around, his cock bobbing slightly, pointing toward the ceiling, Peter's mouth went dry. Luka stalked closer to the bed, and Peter expected him to growl. He loved the way Luka looked, with dark hair on his chest that tapered down his belly. He licked his lips and waited to see what Luka had in mind.

He didn't have to wait long. Luka climbed on the bed, settled between Peter's legs, and used his knees to spread them apart. "You pretty like this," Luka said.

"I'm not pretty. I can be handsome, but I've never been pretty in my life," Peter countered.

Luka grinned evilly, and Peter wondered what he was up to. Then Luka reached out and wrapped his fingers around Peter's length, squeezing, but holding his hand still. Peter flexed his hips to get more friction, but Luka was having none of it. Peter growled.

"Now, that pretty," Luka said.

Peter growled one more time. "That's mean."

Luka gripped him tighter. Peter whimpered and clamped his eyes shut. Then he felt Luka move. With almost painful slowness, Luka stroked him. Peter gasped for air, his mouth hanging open.

Peter snapped his eyes open at the first touch of Luka's lips. Luka took only the head, which nearly drove Peter insane with desire. Desperation built, and he thrust his hips upward, needing more. His every thought centered on his sheer unadulterated urge to race to the finish. He shook with it, but Luka wasn't giving in.

"See? You loved," Luka said.

"More like frustrated," Peter kidded. "Don't tease."

Luka slid his lips farther down. Peter sighed and waited, stilling completely as he willed Luka to give him what he needed. He did… sort of. Peter was nearly out of his mind with desire. If their lovemaking had been under his control, they would probably be done by now. Luka, on the other hand, had patience, and he slowly built the passion inside Peter to the point where he could take no more. Then Luka stopped.

Peter snapped his head forward, darting his gaze around, wondering what happened.

"I am going to love you now," Luka said.

Peter swallowed. "That isn't what you've been doing?"

Luka reached over him to the nightstand and withdrew a condom and a bottle of lube. He set them both nearby and then lifted Peter's legs. Peter watched with rapt attention as Luka slicked his fingers, the clear gel trickling over his digits.

"Luka," Peter whispered when he felt a finger at his entrance. He gasped and then sighed as Luka slid the thick digit carefully into his body. He tensed for a second, tightening his muscles, and then relaxed. Luka took his time, opening him slowly.

Each touch was gentle, yet firm. Peter couldn't remember the last time anyone had treated him with such care. Luka was always wonderful when they were together, but this was different, each touch deeper, more meaningful. When Luka tugged his fingers away, Peter vibrated in anticipation. Luka reached for the condom and rolled it down his shaft. Then he got into position, placed Peter's ankles on his shoulders, and pushed forward.

Peter gritted his teeth at the initial invasion. He relaxed his muscles and breathed a sigh of relief when Luka initially breached him. Taking deep breaths, Peter forced his body to relax rather than spasming at the stretch.

"God," he groaned under a deep breath.

Luka sank deeper, stroking Peter's chest. Their gazes linked and Peter gasped—not at what was happening, but what he saw. He couldn't remember anyone looking at him that way, like he was the center of the very world. Luka filled him, pressing his hips to Peter's butt, and came to a halt. Luka throbbed and jumped inside him. Peter felt every minute movement. He even swore he could feel the beating of Luka's heart.

Then Luka began to move, deliberately.

"Yes," Peter cried.

Once again Luka set his own pace, moving slowly and languidly, rolling his hips rather than snapping them. They moved together, with Luka accompanying their lovemaking with endearments in both Serbian and English. Peter returned them with ones of his own, and soon he was at the limits of his control. His body felt as though it were on fire. Peter stroked himself to Luka's rhythm. Soon he started rolling his head back and forth on the pillow. He gasped for breath as pressure built. Within seconds, Peter clamped his eyes closed as he reached his climax, shooting his release over his stomach and chest.

Warmth spread through him from head to toe. His whole body tingled and then settled into an amazing afterglow that left him floating on clouds. He breathed deeply, afraid to move in case it broke the spell. Slowly, he came back down to earth. Peter opened his eyes and smiled at Luka, who began to move once again.

Luka rolled his hips and quickly picked up speed. Within a minute or so the bed was rocking under him. Sweat rolled down Luka's chest, and the room filled with the musky scent of man. Peter breathed deeply, taking everything in. He knew Luka was close when his rhythm became ragged and his breathing shallow.

"Peter!" Luka cried, and then he thrust deep and then stilled.

Peter felt him coming and saw Luka's eyes drift closed as he throbbed and pulsed deep inside Peter's body. He sat up and reached for Luka, tugging him down. He held Luka tight, letting him catch his breath. He lightly petted Luka's hair. "I love you," he whispered.

"I love you," Luka whispered.

They separated, and Luka took care of the condom before returning to the bed. They held each other until they nearly stuck together. Then Luka got up, took Peter's hand, and led him to the bathroom, where he turned on the shower, and they stepped under the spray for what turned out to be a very sensual shower.

TWO DAYS later, Peter paced the campus sidewalks outside the psychology building. Luka was supposed to meet him here, and Peter was getting antsier by the second. He finally saw Luka approaching, walking past the St. Joan of Arc Chapel. Peter stopped his pacing and waited for Luka to approach.

"Why are you—" Luka shifted back and forth.

"Nervous," Peter supplied, and Luka nodded. "I'm not sure why. I don't know what Franz has planned, and...."

"He is here to help, not hurt. So no be nervous," Luka said and motioned Peter toward the stairs. Peter went inside and up to Franz's office with Luka beside him. He stepped inside, and Franz greeted them both and closed the door behind them. "As I said when we confirmed the appointment, this one will be longer than the others."

Peter nodded. "You remember Luka."

"Of course," Franz said and ushered Luka to one of the chairs in the corner. "You're here mainly for Peter's support."

"Okay," Luka said. Peter watched him settle in the chair and gave him a quick smile before turning back to Franz.

"There's no need to look like you're expecting to be hurt. I promise there are no needles or bad-tasting medicines." Franz pulled his chair from behind the desk and set it right in front of Peter. "What we're going to do is very intimate and can be very revealing. However, you will be outside of your control for a little while, which is why Luka is here. I'd like to hypnotize you." Franz paused. "There will be no parlor tricks. You will not be made to cluck like a chicken or anything as ridiculous as that. Is this agreeable?"

Peter paused, not sure how he felt. Luka stood, walked over to where he sat, and silently placed his hand on his shoulder. Peter placed his hand over Luka's. "All right."

"Very good. It's important for you to know that under hypnosis, your inhibitions and conscious mind take a backseat to memories and feelings that are usually repressed. However, you cannot be compelled to do anything you feel is inherently wrong. So what I want you to do is sit back and get comfortable. When we're done, you are going to feel as though you've gotten a full eight hours sleep. You will also remember everything we have discussed, so nothing will be hidden from you. Do you understand?"

"Yes," Peter answered, squeezing Luka's hand.

Franz shifted his gaze to Luka, and Luka stepped away and took his seat once again. "All right. I want you to listen to the sound of my voice. There's nothing for you to worry about. You are comfortable, warm, and safe. No one is going to interrupt or harm you in any way." Franz's voice was unusually calm and soothing. Within a few minutes, Peter felt himself letting go. He didn't try to stop it even though he knew he could. For some reason he felt empowered, like he was being hypnotized, but he was making it happen rather than having it happen to him.

"Let your head fall forward," Franz said.

Peter did as he was told.

"Good," Franz said in a very soothing voice. "You will remember everything. Do you understand?"

Peter answered, "Yes." He was enjoying the restful state he was in. He heard voices off to the side, but paid no attention to them. They weren't speaking to him, so he continued to relax.

"Very good. What we're going to do is take a trip back into your memory. I want you to think back to when you were six years old. Can you do that?"

"Yes."

"Good. I want you to listen to me. When I tap your knee, you are six years old and in the backyard of the house you grew up in, playing with your brother. You will be there, seeing and feeling everything around you. Do you understand?"

"Yes."

"When I tap your knee, you are six years old, playing in the backyard on the day your brother found the gun. You will not be scared, and nothing bad will happen to you. I want you to remember everything like it was yesterday. You will have no memory blockages and all the details will be available to you. Do you understand?"

"Yes."

"I'm going to count to three. One… two… three…."

Peter felt a tap on his leg, opened his eyes, and looked around. Everything was as he remembered. He stood up and walked toward the swing set in the far corner of the yard.

"Sit back down, Peter. Tell me everything you see, but stay in your chair."

There hadn't been a chair in the backyard, but he sat down in the big-boy chair and looked all around.

"What do you see?"

"Vince and I are playing with a red ball. Dad got it for us yesterday. Awww, Vince…," Peter whined as his brother kicked it into the neighbor's yard. "You gotta get it. Vince!" He pointed, but Vince ignored him.

"What is Vince doing?"

He walked toward the shed to get a pole we saw Dad put in there. "You're not supposed to go in there. You'll get in trouble," he said in a singsongy way. "I followed him. Now Vince has the door open, and I'm going inside too."

"What do you see?"

"Dad never lets us in here, but it's full of machines and carvings. Do you think Dad will give me one for my birthday if I ask him?"

"What's your brother doing?"

"He's climbing on the counter. 'Dad's going to get mad,'" Peter said. "Vince found something." Peter put his hand over his mouth. "It's a gun," Peter said and pressed backward. He didn't want anything to do with it.

"Come on, you baby," Vince told him.

"I am not a baby," Peter said, stamping his foot, but he didn't reach for or take the gun when it was offered to him.

"What's happening?" Franz asked.

"Vince jumped down from the counter and is running around the yard. He's pretending to shoot at the birdies. 'Don't do that, Vince. They're nice birds.'" He paused while Vince called back. "They don't poop everywhere." He put his hands on his head and ran after Vince. "Stop that. You know Dad will be home soon." He looked at the door and wished he could go inside, but Mom had said they were to play in the yard until she called them for dinner.

"What happened next?"

"Vince walked into the shed. I followed him inside," Peter said. "Dad's coming home," Peter added. "Vince hurried by me and closed the door. Now he's trying to climb onto the counter." Peter's heart sped up. "I don't want to see this."

"Be calm and just tell me what happened."

Peter felt a light touch on his hand.

"There's nothing to be afraid of. Just calm down and tell me what you see."

"I'm in the middle of the shed, facing the back. Vince is just in front of me. I can't see the door but I can hear Dad outside. The door is opening. I can see the light coming in." Peter shuddered and put his hands over his ears, closing his eyes. "The gun went off, and I'm falling." He could feel a sharp pain as he landed on his rear end. "It hurts," Peter said and tried to twist around. "The gun is on my lap. I'm picking it up. Ouch." He placed his finger to his lips.

"Daddy is in the doorway staring at me." Peter began to cry and leaped to his feet "Daddy!" He screamed so loud his voice hurt.

"It's okay. I want you to go back to sleep. That was only a memory. You're no longer six. I want you to breathe deeply and relax. Let your head fall forward."

He felt a gentle touch on his head.

"That's very good. Now, when I tap your knee, you will wake up feeling refreshed and rested. You'll also remember everything with no blockage. Three… two… one."

Peter felt a touch on his knee and opened his eyes. The office was there again, and he looked at Franz and then over at Luka.

"How do you feel?"

"Okay, I guess," Peter said.

"What do you remember?"

Peter thought for a few seconds. "Nothing… everything…." He opened his mouth and shivered as everything he'd said and seen rushed back to him. "I didn't do it. I didn't shoot my dad." Peter glanced over at Luka, who was smiling at him. "Vince shot him. He was the one with the gun. He dropped it in my lap, and I picked it up. I couldn't have shot him—my hands were over my ears because of the noise."

Peter turned to Franz, who nodded. Then Peter put his hands over his face and sobbed.

LUKA WAS shocked, beyond shocked. In the back of his mind he'd thought there was something off about Peter's story, but he'd mostly tied that to the fact that Peter had been six years old and had blocked the worst of the incident from his mind. He sat for a few seconds, unable to move, and then stood, hurried to Peter, and wrapped him in his arms. He didn't know what to say, so he said all the things his mother had told him when he was a child. He crooned sweet Serbian nothings into Peter's ear, rocking him back and forth. This man had carried guilt and shame for years, all of it needless. That realization had to be enough to make anyone break down.

"How could he do that?" Peter finally whispered.

No one answered. Dr. Middlebach handed Luka a tissue, and he pressed it into Peter's hand.

"It is okay," Luka said softly. "Answers come in time."

"Your friend is right," the doctor said softly. "Peter, I want you to look at me."

Luka took a single small step back and to the side.

"You honestly thought you'd shot your father, and we were able to unlock your memories. But I want to caution you that you need to think about what you wish to do with this information."

"Why?" Peter snapped. "My brother shot Dad. He knew it all these years and he let me take the fall. He let me think I'd done it and feel guilty for it for decades." Peter shook, and Luka stepped closer, taking his hand.

"You were both children, six and eight years old," Franz said. "Your recovered memory doesn't change the end result. It only shifts the guilt." Franz stood up.

Luka moved and sat back down. He watched as Franz knelt near Peter.

"You need to decide what you want to do with this information."

Peter lifted his gaze, and slowly the doctor returned to his chair.

"I don't understand," Peter said. "Why would I tell my family? They...." Peter paused and nodded slowly. "They wouldn't believe me."

"What I'm saying is that you just found out something life-changing. But the most important person whose life it will change is yours. For years you've carried this guilt, something you now know you don't need to do. It will change who you are. The residual guilt will dissipate, and you'll be free of it."

"That's a good thing, isn't it?" Peter asked.

"Yes. It is good. But that guilt was also responsible for some of the wonderful things in your life. I know it sounds strange, but that guilt pushed you to help people and to become the person you are. Without it, you will change. Your personality will shift, maybe slightly, maybe a whole lot. That depends on you." The doctor leaned forward in his chair. "Like I said, what you do with this information is up to you. But I suggest you think about it and give yourself a chance to adjust."

Peter looked shocked. Luka wanted to go to him, but thought it best to sit back and let the doctor talk with Peter, especially as he explained potential changes. Luka knew people changed and grew, but the thought of Peter becoming anyone other than the incredible man he'd come to love shook him to the core.

"So I should do nothing?" Peter asked, pulling Luka out of his thoughts.

"For now. The most important thing is that you know the truth about what happened. Give yourself a chance to digest it and decide what is best for you." Franz looked at Luka as well. "Then you can decide with the important people in your life what you want to do. Things like this can cause a great deal of trauma for both the person affected and the people around them. We've discovered the truth together, now let's determine the best way forward together."

Peter took a deep breath and sighed. "Okay. I think I can do that. But should I not tell anyone?"

"My suggestion would be to pick a few close friends and tell them the whole story. That way you will have a support group of understanding people. Don't tell your family, and definitely not your brother, until you're absolutely ready. The truth has been hidden for a very long time. But you're in control of it now, so give yourself the chance to heal and to be strong before you entrust that truth to others."

Peter sighed again and nodded.

"People not always believe the truth," Luka said.

Peter turned toward him. "Do you believe me?"

Luka smiled and walked over to Peter, took his hand, and placed it on his chest. "With whole heart."

"I believe that Luka believed there was more to the story before either of us did," Franz said, and Luka nodded.

"I know you could not hurt anyone," Luka said.

Peter stood up, still holding Luka's hand.

"I'd like to schedule an appointment on Monday," Franz said. "That will give you some time to think, and we can then talk over what you'd like to do." He paused. "I want to caution you that you're likely to feel a number of strong emotions over the next few days. Please do not act on them. They're normal, but acting on them will most likely lead you to consequences you don't mean or intend. Okay?"

Peter nodded.

Franz stood up as well. "Feel free to call if you need to talk. I'll be here to listen."

Peter thanked him, and Luka did as well. Peter seemed tentative as he walked toward the door, so Luka stayed close to him. Once they were out of the building and into the fresh air, Peter seemed to steady. He led them to a shady spot under a tree and stood in the shade, taking deep, long breaths. Luka waited patiently while Peter looked up at the leaves and clear sky overhead.

"I feel like a weight has been lifted off my shoulders and I can't tell anyone."

Luka remained quiet.

"All these years I thought I was the one who had killed my father, and Vince let me think it." Peter lowered his gaze. "Do you think he knew all this time?"

Luka shrugged.

"How could he do that?" Peter asked, clenching his fists. "I want to hit him." He then laughed nervously. "I suppose that's why Franz asked me to think about things." He ran his hands through his hair. "What am I going to do?"

"I do not know. What you want to do?" Luka asked. He tried to figure out how he'd feel if he were in Peter's place and came up blank.

"I've been living a lie since I was six years old," Peter said. "For twenty-five years, I've thought I killed my father and I didn't. I lived with that guilt and shame all that time, needlessly. What happened was not my fault, and yet I paid for it." He began pacing in the shade.

"I think we go home," Luka said. "You need to think."

Peter stopped and nodded. Then he strode down the sidewalk, and Luka struggled to keep up. "Peter," Luka said, and Peter slowed down to allow Luka to catch up. Luka could feel the energy rolling off Peter in waves. They walked to Peter's car, and Peter drove them to his apartment. Milton greeted them at the door. The cat took one look at Peter, growled, and hurried away.

"Coward," Peter cried after the cat as he shut the door.

"You need to... relax," Luka said. "You cannot change anything right now."

"But everything is different," Peter said.

"No. Everything the same. Only difference is you know the truth now," Luka said. "You no longer have guilty feelings, but you are still finding your way." Luka walked into the kitchen and found Milton's food. He put some in the bowl, and the cat approached, walking near the wall, slinking around Peter before attacking his dish. "He know something wrong."

Peter didn't say anything. He walked over to the sofa and flopped down. "I can't believe I didn't remember that I didn't do it. I didn't kill my dad." Peter smiled and then began to shake. "How could I not remember that all these years?"

"It was scary and...." Luka groaned and switched to Serbian. "You were young and your father had just been shot with the gun you and your brother had found. Your mind couldn't process everything, so it blocked things out. The last thing you remembered was holding the gun. Everyone else saw you with the gun, so they concluded you had accidentally shot your dad, and since you couldn't remember, you didn't deny it." Luka sat next to Peter. "I'm sorry you went through all that, but if you hadn't, I wouldn't have met you and you wouldn't be the man you are today."

"How can you say that?" Peter asked.

It would be easier to continue in Serbian, but Luka switched to English and hoped he could say what he wanted without tripping over his words. "You are the man I love... the person you are... because you think you killed your dad. You help people. If that not happen, you might be lawyer or guy who wires houses, not social worker or person who teach me English."

Peter seemed to settle down a little. "I know. But I've felt so bad for so long."

"Yes. But that be over if you let it be over," Luka said, hoping he was explaining himself well. "You need... forgive, just like you wanted family to forgive."

Peter sighed. "I know you're right, but that's much easier said than done." Milton wandered over and jumped on the sofa. Peter must not have been scary to him now because he immediately rubbed all over both of them. "I know Franz is right, but I'm going to go crazy unless I can talk about it."

Luka lifted his hands away from Milton and crossed his arms over his chest. "Then talk if you want. I listen."

Peter ran his hands through his hair. "I didn't mean to make you mad. Everything seems all messed up. The things I thought I knew aren't what I thought they were."

Luka remained quiet and let Peter talk.

"Maybe I'm making too much of this whole thing. Yes, I didn't shoot my dad, but I was still there, and…."

"You think too much," Luka said with a smile. "Just be happy. You no can bring back father, but you know you not kill him. That good news. So be happy. Forgive and go on with life." Luka smiled. "It like you said." Luka waved his hands over his head. "Universe in balance." Luka smiled. "Is that right?"

"Yes," Peter said with a smile. "That's right." He reached over and pulled Luka to him. "I'll do what Franz suggested and think about it for a while."

"Good." Luka shifted closer. Milton mrowed and jumped to the floor as Luka angled closer for a kiss. "I no want you to change," Luka whispered, giving voice to what Franz had said earlier.

"I don't plan on it," Peter said.

"Good. I like you like this," Luka said, and then he cut off further conversation for a while. They rolled together on the couch. In Luka's mind, what was important was being close to each other, not sex. Neither of them pressed for it, and that was fine. Being there for each other was more important.

"Can I ask something?" Peter said, his lips swollen and red from their kissing. Luka nodded. "Do you still miss Misha?"

Luka nodded again. "I will always miss him. I still love him. Just like I would still love and miss you if something happened." The thought made Luka shiver. He did not want to go through that kind of pain again, ever. "He's a part of me, just like you are." Luka smiled. "You… I no know the word. But you have green eyes," Luka said.

"I do not," Peter said. "And the word is jealous, which I'm not, thank you very much." Peter ran his fingers over Luka's ribs. He laughed and squirmed before diving in to tickle Peter back. They wriggled and laughed until they ended up on the floor with Luka on top of Peter, both of them laughing like idiots. It was so good to hear Peter laugh a genuine, carefree laugh.

"If you not jealous, then why ask about Misha?" Luka asked, shifting to get back on his feet.

Peter wrapped his arms around his waist and held him still. "I was curious. It must be hard to lose someone like that."

"Everyone loses someone," Luka said. "You lost your dad, and Bella lost Josif. It what happens. I love Misha and I miss him, like I miss Josif. But you no stop living. Misha would be mad at me if I did that."

"Is that what kept you going?"

"Yes. Misha was... fun, lively. He always moving. So that how I know he is angry if I sit and do nothing. And I no want Misha to be mad. He say he come back and make me pay if I not remember him right."

"He said he'd haunt you? Like a ghost?" Peter asked.

Luka nodded. "He want me to be happy. Like I want you to be happy. Anger, jealous, hate—all make you unhappy. They not healthy. Need to let them go to be happy." Luka stroked Peter's cheek. "You need to let go to be happy."

Peter hummed softly. "You make me happy."

Luka smiled. "Yes. But you need to make you happy too."

"Is this your way of telling me to let go of what Vince did?" Peter asked. Luka sat on the floor and shook his head. "Then what are you telling me?"

"To be happy. I no understand what that is, but you have to do that. Yell at him if want, punch in nose, scream if that make you feel better. But you need to decide what that is. Do it once, and then walk away. He still brother and only one you have."

"So you're telling me not to burn my bridges," Peter said.

Luka nodded. He thought he understood what Peter was saying. That expression was new, but the image worked for him. "You know truth and that enough for now. Rest will come later."

"You sound like Franz," Peter observed.

"Franz is right," Luka said. "What you think happen if you tell Mama what you remember? She open arms and hug you?" Luka shook his head. "She say you liar and get angry with you. That what happen with long lie. It become truth. You must think for long time before telling anybody. I know you want to tell Mama, but that not help."

"I know," Peter agreed. "After the shooting, my mother was different. I have memories of her reading to me at bedtime and kissing me when I got hurt. After Dad died, that all stopped. She spent extra time with Vince and Julie, but not me. I wanted her to. I was a little kid and I wanted my mother to tell me everything would be okay. I know she blamed me for what happened, but I was a little kid who needed his mother. I didn't get it, so I hoped if I was good, she would love me again."

Luka nodded. "Maybe your mother feel guilty. Maybe she want to forgive but don't know how."

"Maybe." Peter chuckled. "You met my mother. She knows what she knows, and it is very hard for her to change her mind." He sighed. "Okay. You made your point, whether you wanted to or not. I won't say anything to anyone until I figure out how I feel about all this."

"Good," Luka said. "I need to go home."

"You do?" Peter asked.

"I promised Bella I would have dinner with her. She need company, and I promise to eat with her." He smiled. "She asked you to come too if want."

"Are you sure?" Peter asked.

Luka nodded, rolling his eyes. No one got Bella to do something she didn't want to do.

"Did she really invite me?"

"Yes. She want people to talk to, and she just go back to work." Luka grinned. "She say she is ready to be out with people."

"If you're sure. I'd like to see Bella and have dinner. She was always a really good cook," Peter said, patting his stomach. They got off the floor, and Peter went to the bathroom. When he returned, he locked the apartment, and they left for Luka's.

The short drive to Luka's didn't take long. When Peter parked in his usual place, Bella came out of the main house and hurried over to them. "There was a man here looking for you," she said and handed Luka a card. Luka read it, his heart going cold. "US Citizenship and Immigration Service."

"What did they want?" Peter asked.

She shook her head. "He wouldn't say. Only that he wanted to speak with Luka and that it was important."

"What are they?" Luka asked.

"They're the department that allowed you to come to this country. They decide if you can stay or if you have to go back to Serbia," Peter explained.

"I cannot go back," Luka said. "I left everything behind and...." He shivered at the thought of the reception he'd receive if he were forced to return. Because he'd left in the first place, his life would turn to a veritable hell. The government would not be happy he'd left and would not welcome him back with open arms. "What we do?" Luka asked, swallowing hard.

"We find out what they want," Bella said. "They would tell me nothing at all."

"Do we call now?" Luka asked, his insides churning with fear.

"We can try," Peter offered. Luka unlocked the door to his apartment and the others followed him inside. He called the number on the card, but only got a voice mail recording. He thought about leaving a message but hung up instead.

"No answer," he said. He shoved his phone into his pocket and it began to chime. He pulled it out and answered it. "Hello."

"I just missed a call from this number," a masculine voice asked.

"I'm Luka Krachek, I was told to call." He glanced at Bella and Peter. "Who this?"

"Marvin Weston from USCIS," the man answered.

Luka felt Peter touch the small of his back.

"We have your paperwork requesting a permanent work permit and green card." Luka already had a temporary work permit, which he kept in a safe place. "Everything seems to be in order, except a couple of items have come to light. The first is that the relative sponsoring you is no longer living."

"Yes," Luka confirmed. He didn't hear anything after that. All he could think about was that they were going to send him back because Josif had died.

"Mr. Krachek, are you still there?"

"Yes. I here," Luka said. "His wife, Bella, can she sponsor me?"

"Yes…."

Luka didn't wait, he handed Bella the phone.

"I'm Bella Krachek, the widow of Josif Krachek, and I'm willing to sponsor Luka," she said into the phone, then listened. "Yes, he has a job. You should have the employment information. He also has a place to live. You saw it when you were here today." She listened once more, and Luka began biting his nails. "Of course. That isn't a problem. Luka has valuable skills that this country will benefit from. I'm sure his colleagues at the university will be able to provide the information you need. Send the forms and a request for all the information you need. We'll complete them and get them returned to you right away." Bella flashed Luka a quick smile. "Very good. I'm going to put Luka back on the phone." She handed it to him. "It's okay," she soothed.

Luka breathed a sigh of relief. "Hello," he said.

"We're going to send you and your cousin the appropriate forms to be filled out and signed. They will have to be notarized, but all that will be explained in the instructions. Provided you can give us the information and everything is in order, I don't see an issue on that front." Luka sighed. Marvin spoke quickly, but Luka thought he understood most of what he'd said.

"I understand," Luka said.

"Good. Now there is one other issue. We have received a statement from the Serbian authorities asserting that you…," he said, drawing out the last word, "… are in possession of property that belongs to the Serbian government. They are requesting your return to that country."

"I did not steal anything," Luka said more loudly than he intended. "I work for the government in Serbia before I came here. I know things they not want me to tell."

"I see," Weston said. "Okay. Let me look into this a little further. In the meantime, complete and return the paperwork. Don't leave the country, and please remain where we can contact you."

"I will," Luka said. He wasn't sure what else to ask, so he thanked the man and hung up.

"What happened?" Peter asked, placing an arm around his waist.

"I think they're trying to get me to go back," Luka said.

"That won't happen," Bella told him. "Here, they have no authority. We'll fill out the paperwork as soon as they send it, get it signed and notarized, and send it back to them. You have a job where you're valued—that will go a long way."

"But what if they make trouble?" Luka asked.

"That's what they're trying to do. But the government here doesn't like to be pushed around." Bella patted his shoulder. "Try to relax and not think about it too much. When you go to work tomorrow, tell your boss what is happening. His support in completing the paperwork will help." Bella walked toward the door. "I need to get dinner out of the oven. You two talk for a few minutes and then come over." She opened the door and stepped out, leaving the two of them alone.

"Why is nothing ever easy?" Peter asked.

Luka looked at him and nodded. "I thought when I out of Serbia everything be fine. I start new life here and I be happy." Luka moved closer to Peter. "I not complaining, but I think things be easy here."

Peter chuckled softly. "Since I was a kid, I wished I hadn't shot my dad. I just learned today that I didn't. I got what I wanted, or part of what I wanted. But it doesn't seem to matter like I thought it would."

Luka hummed his agreement and rested his head on Peter's chest. "You got me."

"That I did. And that's the best thing that has ever happened to me." Peter angled to kiss him. "I will not let them send you back. I know that's what you're worried about, but it won't happen. We won't let it." Peter kissed him lightly. "I waited my entire life for someone as wonderful as you, and I won't let anyone take you away."

Luka hoped Peter was right. The thought of leaving filled him with dread. After losing Misha, he hadn't expected to find someone to care for and who cared for him like Peter. Certainly not as quickly as he had. He was lucky. Yes, part of him still grieved for Misha, but his heart was open, and Peter made him happy. Now if only it wasn't ripped away from him.

THEY HAD a quiet dinner at Bella's. She and Peter held up most of the conversation, with Peter sharing his story and the hypnotic revelation that he'd spent decades believing he'd accidentally shot his father, but hadn't. Bella had agreed with Luka and said he should indeed think about what he wanted and that he might even consider keeping the information to himself.

Luka listened, but rarely spoke. His mind was on the earlier phone call. "Do you think they try to force me to go back?" he finally asked toward the end of the meal. He couldn't get the earlier phone call out of his mind.

"I don't think so, but we will do our best to stop them if they try," Bella said, and Peter nodded, placing a hand on Luka's knee. "You came here with permission from the government of this country. That's what really counts. None of us lied or were deceitful when we asked permission and applied for the temporary work permit through the university. So they have no basis to make you leave. We need to get the permanent paperwork started, and that is what is being sent. I don't think you have anything to worry about." Bella patted his hand.

Luka looked to Peter for reassurance. "I agree with Bella," Peter said softly, but Luka saw fear in his eyes.

"You two need to think positively," Bella said and then began to laugh. "That's great advice coming from me, the woman who broke down into tears this morning because I burned the toast." Bella reached for her napkin and wiped her eyes. "I'm not sure if it's the hormones or Josif, but I cry at the drop of a hat."

"Maybe it both," Luka offered. "You cry if you want."

Bella huffed and sniffed.

"How was work?" Peter asked

"Sucky," Bella answered. "Everyone treated me like I was glass, and when I told them I was pregnant, most people were thrilled, but others looked at me like I was some poor little match girl."

"What that mean?" Luka asked Peter.

"Pity," Peter said, and Luka nodded.

"They felt sorry for me that Josif was gone and then because I was going to be a single mother. I wanted to pull the bitches' hair out." Bella stared at Luka.

"It not only crying," Luka said. "I not mess with you."

"Damn straight," Bella said and then smiled. Luka glanced at Peter and then back at Bella, wondering if she was okay. "It's just everything. Sometimes I cry, and sometimes I have this urge to hurt people who piss me off." She sat back, rubbing her belly. "I want this baby more than anything."

Peter glanced at him. "We know."

"Any more from doctor?" Luka asked.

"Not yet," Bella answered. "But I know he's okay." She swallowed, and Luka thought she was going to cry again. "Josif came to me in a dream and told me the baby was fine and that it was going to be a boy." She lifted her napkin and used it to dab her eyes. "I know it sounds crazy, but I want to believe it's true."

"Of course you do," Peter said. "And there's nothing wrong with believing that Josif is looking out for you." His voice broke. "I used to wish my dad was looking out for me. I didn't think I deserved it because of what had happened and all, but I used to wish it." He shrugged. "Maybe he was. Maybe my dad was looking out for me and helping me all these years. I grew up and made it on my own somehow."

Bella nodded, but said nothing. Eventually Peter changed the subject and they began discussing baby names. That morphed into each of them listing the most unusual names they knew, which brought laughter when Peter mentioned Lemonjello. Luka asked him to explain the joke, and Bella got a box and placed it on the table. Finally he understood and laughed along with the others.

It was dark by the time they left. Bella turned on the lights in the yard, and Peter and Luka walked to Luka's place. Inside, Luka locked the door, and they went through the dim apartment to the stairs and then up to the bedroom.

"I don't want to have to leave," Luka said into the darkness.

"You won't," Peter whispered. "We both deserve some happiness, and I'm convinced that for me, you are happiness."

He hugged Luka tight and kissed him hard. When they were together, their kisses were usually tender and soft, but not tonight. Peter was forceful, each kiss searingly deep. Luka felt his knees go weak and pressed harder to Peter in order to keep himself upright. Once they moved closer to the bed, Peter began yanking at Luka's clothes. They broke their kisses only long enough for Peter to pull Luka's shirt over his head. After that it was a dash to skin. Peter had Luka's clothes off and him on the bed within seconds.

The energy coming off Peter carried an almost electric buzz. Within seconds, Luka was on fire. He began pulling at Peter's clothes. Soon they were skin to skin. Luka sighed, and Peter roamed his hands all over Luka's body, chest, belly, arms, sides, then cupped his butt. They didn't stop for long, and neither did the vibrations that didn't seem to end.

"Peter," Luka said, his voice rough.

"I'm scared," Peter whispered, his face near Luka's ear.

"Me too," Luka admitted. He wanted to think he was overreacting or being stupid, but in his heart he knew he could be asked to leave, and something deep inside said if they did, he wouldn't be given much time. His mother used to say that only God knew how much time they had. His mother had been right.

Luka tightened his hold on Peter and gave himself over to their lovemaking, letting it stop his mind and push away the rest of the world. His worries and fears slipped away, replaced by body-shaking passion. He wanted to hold, taste, and feel Peter for the rest of his life, and from the way Peter held him, pressing them together from toes to chest, he wanted the same thing.

"Love you," Peter whispered. He rubbed their cocks along each other, the room filling with their whimpers and moans.

Within minutes, Luka was soaring outside of himself. Pressure built and abated only to build again. Luka hoped this would never end. He stroked up and down Peter's back, over the curve of his tight butt, and then up once again toward his shoulders.

"Love you too," Luka said.

Peter kissed him and then sank down his body, licking and kissing as he went. Luka arched his back, pushing his chest into the delightful pressure, desperate for more. He needed and wanted it so desperately he could hardly think. "I need!"

"I know," Peter told him. "And I'll give it to you, I promise. But not yet. I want you to always remember that you're mine. I love you for always, and no matter what, I will not let you go."

Luka thought for a few seconds: What would Peter do if he were forced to leave? He wanted to ask, but then Peter lightly pinched a nipple before sucking his length between his lips. After that, the world narrowed to only him and Peter. Nothing else mattered. Not his worries or his fears. They were gone. Only Peter existed, at least for now.

Peter sucked him hard and deep, the sensation mind-blowingly good. Luka hissed and groaned louder and louder as Peter continued sucking. He didn't want to come, not yet, but he was fast approaching the point of no return. Luka tried to signal, but it was already too late. He was floating and soaring within seconds as he came hard and fast, throbbing in the back of Peter's throat.

Luka collapsed back onto his mattress, trying to make his mind work. But he gave up and let himself fly on the wings of afterglow. He felt Peter shift and lie down beside him, but he couldn't move and didn't try. Open-mouthed, breathing steadily, he willingly basked in the warmth of Peter's love. He knew that was what he felt. Luka hadn't felt this wonderful since Misha, but he recognized the feeling. He was completely and totally in love with Peter.

That thought stayed with him as the worries crept around the edges. How would he feel and what would he do if he were forced to leave? How on earth could he leave Peter and still keep his heart intact? The answer hit him hard: he couldn't. If he had to leave, his heart would shatter. Peter had become very important to him. He believed in him, supported him.

"Why are you smiling, besides the obvious?" Peter asked with a small chuckle.

"I was just thinking about you." Luka rolled on his side and then climbed on top of Peter. He grinned as he straddled him, staring down at Peter's half-lidded eyes.

"What did you have in mind?" Peter asked. Luka stretched toward the nightstand and pulled out the supplies. He rolled a condom down Peter's length, lubed his fingers, and prepared himself before lifting himself and then slowly lowering his body onto Peter.

Peter gasped and groaned, pressing up into him. Luka tried to control their joining as best he could, but he figured Peter was way too far gone for control. Luka held still, and Peter thrust up into him. Luka cried out and met Peter's movements with his own, settling across Peter's hips.

Luka waited a few moments and then rolled his hips, slow and long, listening to Peter's small moans. He did it again and again, stretching his body so Peter could get a good look. Peter placed his hands on Luka's hips and began to move. Luka raised himself and dropped once again before lifting himself and holding still. Peter began to move under him, thrusting upward, deeper and deeper. He held Luka's hips tightly to steady him and moved faster and faster. Luka watched as Peter's eyes glaze over.

They moved together, Luka matching Peter's thrusts. He tightened his muscles, and Peter hissed. Then Luka sank down and gripped Peter as hard as he could.

"Luka!" Peter cried, thrusting upward, lifting him. Then Peter stilled as he throbbed deep inside him.

Neither of them moved. Peter closed his eyes and lay back on the mattress, breathing deeply. Luka groaned and slowly lifted off Peter's body. Then he settled on the mattress and held Peter close, letting him ride through his pleasure.

"You're amazing," Peter finally said. "I thought you were going to kill me."

"No kill. Want you around for a long time." Luka closed his eyes and snuggled closer for a few minutes, until Peter got up and took care of the remnants of their lovemaking. Then he returned to the bed and they moved close together. Luka got the sense that after this very unsettling day for both of them, they both needed to be held.

"It be okay," Luka said.

"I was going to tell you the same thing," Peter said. Luka nodded and decided to try his best to take his own advice. Worrying wouldn't do either of them any good.

"I don't want to leave," Luka said, giving voice to his fear.

"I don't want you to leave. So we'll need to stay together and fight if necessary. Bella was right on both accounts: we'll do everything we can to make sure you stay, and I promise to think long and hard before I do anything about telling my family. Until then, I suggest we both get some sleep, because I think we're going to need our rest. The next week or so is going to be very busy." Peter pulled him closer, and Luka closed his eyes, hoping his happiness wouldn't be short-lived.

PETER KNEW he was dreaming; he had to be, because he was sitting on his sofa, watching television, and his father walked in from the kitchen and sat beside him. "What are you doing here, Dad?" Peter asked. He looked just the same as Peter remembered, well, at least partially. He hadn't realized how much he looked like his father until this very second. They had the same eyes and nose. If Peter cut his hair as short as his father's, they could have passed for twins.

"I came because I think you need my help," his father said and sat down beside him, patting his knee once. "What happened wasn't your fault, and it wasn't your brother's fault."

"But, Dad, he shot you and let me think I'd done it," Peter said.

His father shook his head. "There's only one person to blame for what happened to me, and that's me. Yes, your brother should have fessed up to what he did years ago, and that needs to be put right, for both your sakes. But the person truly responsible for my death was me. I was the one who bought that damned gun. Your mother nearly killed me and refused to let me keep it in the house. I didn't remember that it was loaded when I put it away, but I should have checked." The sadness in his father's eyes was palpable. "You see, I should have known that with two young boys and your sister around the house, one of you would find the thing." His father paused.

"Dad, they never forgave me for what happened," Peter said. "I've lived with that for all these years." He paused and blinked at the image of his father. He knew he couldn't possibly be speaking with him.

"You never forgave yourself, son." His father turned away. "I should have come to you earlier. I know that now. But you're a lot stronger than you give yourself credit for."

"Why now, Dad?" Peter asked. "Why come to me now and not years ago when I really needed you?"

His father stood up and took a step back toward the kitchen. "None of us gets to choose our time, including me. I wish I'd had more of it with all of you. But I didn't. How you handle what you know will determine how much time you have with your brother and sister. They're the ones you need to build the relationship with. There's plenty of blame and guilt on all sides, especially with me." His father took another step and disappeared. Peter jumped off the sofa and caught his legs in something. He began to fall and hit the floor.

"Peter," Luka called.

He opened his eyes and blinked. He was in Luka's bedroom, sprawled out on the floor, Luka peering over the side of the mattress. "I'm okay," he whispered and blinked a few more times, trying to figure out what had happened. It had been a dream. Hell, it had to have been a dream.

"What happened?" Luka asked as Peter climbed back in the bed.

"I was just having a dream," Peter answered. Luka hummed and moved close. Within seconds he seemed to have gone back to sleep, but Peter remained awake for quite a while.

HE WOKE what seemed like way too early on Monday morning and went in to work after his appointment with Franz. He spent his day either with clients or pushing paperwork, all the while helping people navigate the social services bureaucracy. Over the weekend, he'd taught his language class, and Luka had gone with him. That evening they had planned to spend more time together working on

Luka's language skills, but when he finally arrived at Luka's, he found him sitting at his table with a mound of forms in front of him.

"Help me," Luka said, holding up one of the government forms.

"Of course," Peter said, placing the materials he'd brought aside. "Why don't we get Bella to help too?"

Luka got up and went to get Bella while Peter began sorting through the forms. There were some Luka would need the university to complete for him while others needed to be completed by Bella, as his sponsor. The task was daunting, and once Bella arrived, they divided and conquered. After a while, Peter ordered dinner, and they continued working, dissecting Luka's past work life and family history. By the time they had done all they could, Luka was a nervous wreck. Though he and Bella were exhausted, they seemed to have made a lot of progress. Peter could understand Luka's jitteriness. He understood the basic government processes, but to Luka all this probably seemed like a black hole he was descending into with no way out and no end in sight.

"Okay," Bella said, leaning over the table. "I've got everything organized. We need to take these to be notarized. They can probably help you with that at the university when you take these forms in to human resources." Bella had color-coded everything based upon who had to do what. "That's the red. The yellow you need to sign, and they go with the red forms once they're notarized. The blue ones I have nearly completed, and I need to send those in. I'll have them notarized and get them sent tomorrow." Bella sat back, slowly rubbing her belly. "There's nothing for you to worry about."

"But the news on television…," Luka said.

Peter knew he'd heard stories about the debate going on regarding immigration.

"You came here legally," Bella reminded him. "I'm sure this is only the first round of documentation, but you have a good job and skills that this country needs. The reason we did all this is so we can provide them with the information they need to make the right decision." Bella pushed back her chair and yawned before standing up. "Tomorrow we will call the man from customs and immigration and find out the rest of what's going on." She patted Luka's shoulder and then walked toward the door.

"She...," Luka began, but didn't finish.

"Yes. She's something else. After all she's been though...." Peter swallowed. "Josif was a good man, and they loved each other."

"They did," Luka agreed.

"Will you be angry when she finds someone else?" Peter asked, and Luka snapped his head around until he faced him. "Not right away, of course, but she's going to find someone else to love." Peter reached across the table and took Luka's hand, "Just like you found me."

"I think *you* found *me,*" Luka said.

Peter shook his head. "You were the one who found me. I was dead inside and had been for a long time. There was nothing but guilt and pain. But you changed that. Yes, Franz helped me remember what happened, but it was you who took the chance that got me the help I needed. I yelled at you for it, and for that I'm sorry." He could see things clearly now, things he'd never seen before. "You did what you did because you cared."

"There are lots of people who care," Luka said.

"I know that now," Peter said. Then he looked down at his old cell phone sitting on the table. He picked it up. "I think I need to make a call." He had decided, with the help of Franz earlier that day, what he wanted to do, and it was time. Luka nodded, and Peter stood up and stepped outside.

Late summer air with a hint of crispness greeted him when he closed the door. Peter looked up into the canopy of leaves that hung overhead. He shuffled down the walk to the wooden swing under one of the trees. He sat and dialed the familiar number.

"Hi, Mom," he said when she answered.

"It's Julie," his sister said. "Mom's lying down. They did the cataract surgery today in her left eye. They said she's doing well and were very hopeful."

"That's really good. I just called to see how she was doing. She told me they wanted to do the procedure, but she didn't say when."

"It wasn't supposed to be until next week, but they had an opening and she figured it was now or never. You know Mom— once she makes up her mind, there's no changing it." The line went quiet.

"How are you holding up?" Peter asked.

"I'm fine. She'll be okay. She'll need to wear dark glasses for a while, but once this eye is healed, they'll do the other one and then she'll be as good as new," Julie explained.

"Excellent," Peter said, looking up into the trees as a breeze rustled the leaves. "Tell Mom I'll be over to see her after I get out of work tomorrow."

"I will," Julie said.

They hung up, and Peter wondered exactly what he was going to say to his mother. They'd been virtual strangers for such a long time. Even when he was still living at home, he'd felt like a stranger to his own mother. Peter started slightly when Luka sat down next to him. He hadn't heard him approach.

"You make up your mind?" Luka asked.

"Yes. I've decided they need to know the truth, but without accusations or guilt. There's been enough of that already. I thought about saying nothing, but if I do that, then nothing will change." Peter sighed and slowly began to move the swing with his feet. "They need to know the truth, but I think I need to start with Vince. He needs to know that I know what really happened." Peter turned toward Luka. "I don't blame him for anything now, and I think he needs to know that. I suspect Vince has been carrying around a great deal of guilt and pain, just like I was. He was better at hiding it."

"Then you call him," Luka said and settled back in the swing. He didn't move closer and said nothing. Peter knew he was there, keeping him company, being there in case he was needed. After thinking for a few minutes, Peter looked up the number in his contacts.

"Vince, it's Peter," he said when he heard his brother's familiar voice. There was quite a commotion in the background.

"Hi, Peter," Vince said. The high-pitched squeals came through the phone. "It's bath time." The line went quiet and then Vince returned. "Margaret is watching them," he said, and the background noise quieted.

Peter wondered how he should do this, but figured direct was best. "I was wondering if I could see you tomorrow afternoon. I have to come up to see Mom, and I thought I would swing by on my way, if that's all right." He tried to sound casual.

Vince paused. "Sure, that would be fine. About five thirty?"

"That'd be great," Peter said.

"I gotta get back. Those two can be a handful."

"Of course. I'll see you tomorrow," Peter said. He hung up and placed the phone next to him on the seat before closing his eyes. "What am I doing?" he asked the tree above him.

"I no understand," Luka said from next to him.

"I don't either," Peter whispered. "I want to talk to him, but I'm afraid of hurting his life and his little girls. Vince is happy and he deserves to be. Is dredging up the past really worth it?"

"Only you can answer," Luka said. "You know truth. Is that enough?"

Peter wanted it to be. He really did. But it wasn't. He wished he could forget the years of guilt and regret he'd suffered, but he couldn't.

"What did doctor say?" Luka asked.

Peter chuckled. "We went back and forth, but he didn't offer any advice in the end other than to do what I thought best. I only wish I knew what that was." Peter's head ached.

"You do know," Luka told him. "What you want to be told is you are right. And no one can tell you that. You have to make your decision and know you are doing what is best. I cannot tell and no one else can. If you want to talk to Vince and your mother, I go with you."

Peter wasn't so sure that was a good idea. But the more he thought about it, the better it sounded to him. He could at least keep his family from yelling and screaming. "Thank you." Peter stood up and placed his phone back in his pocket. "I need to go home. I think it's best if I have some time to myself." He leaned closer, kissing Luka. "I need time to think."

Luka nodded and kissed him again. Then Peter went inside, gathered his things, and got in his car. He said good-bye to Luka, who was still sitting on the swing. He hated to leave, but he needed his mind clear, and it rarely was with Luka around. Whatever he did, he needed to handle things gently. The truth might set you free, but in this case, Peter was sure his family wouldn't be willing to accept the truth.

PETER SLEPT very little that night. He spent most of the time staring at the ceiling and running through scenarios and conversations with his brother and mother. Of course he got nowhere, and finally in the wee hours of the morning, he fell asleep. Peter got up when his alarm sounded, showered, fed Milton, and went in to work. He was jumpy for much of the day. Thankfully it was quiet. At the end of the day, he drove to Luka's and picked him up, and then they were on their way to Vince's.

The drive took half an hour, and then he pulled into his brother's driveway. The yard was quiet. Peter led Luka up the walk and knocked on the door. Vince opened it and motioned for them to be quiet. "We just got the twins down for their nap. They've been fighting Margaret all afternoon." He opened the door, and they stepped inside. Vince closed the door and led them through the house and down the stairs to his man cave in the basement. He motioned them to the large leather chairs. "Was there something you wanted to talk about?"

Peter got jumpy and moved to the edge of the chair. "I've been seeing a psychologist for the past few weeks. There have been things in my life that I have found difficult to deal with, and one of those things was Dad's death." Peter figured he'd tread lightly at first.

Vince nodded. "I regret that day as well."

"The thing is, the doctor helped me recover some memories I didn't know I had. I've always thought I shot Dad. But I didn't. I ended up with the gun after the shot was fired." Peter said nothing more and waited to see what Vince would do.

Vince said nothing for a full minute. "I know you didn't shoot Dad. I did." He stood up and strode over to the bar in the corner. He returned with bottles of beer and popped them open, then handed them out to Peter and Luka before downing most of his own. "It was an accident."

"I know," Peter said.

"After the gun went off, I dropped it and you picked it up. When people rushed in, everyone thought you had done it, and you never denied it. I know I should have said something, and for years wished I had. Then it became clear you didn't remember, and it got easier and easier to just keep it to myself." Vince finished his beer and opened another.

"I'm not here to place blame or to rehash who did what. I've spent days going from angry to hurt and finally resigned. I debated saying anything at all, but that wasn't an option. You see, I spent decades feeling guilty for what I'd thought I'd done." Peter found himself struggling. "Then last night I thought maybe you had felt the same kind of guilt I had."

Vince nodded, holding the bottle between his hands.

"But there isn't any blame. It was an accident, like you said."

"But I still killed my father," Vince said, breaking down in a way Peter had never seen before.

"Like I said, it was an accident, and if anyone is to blame, it's Dad," Peter said. "For years I thought in huge circles about what I did. If we hadn't been in the shed and hadn't found the gun, nothing would have happened and Dad wouldn't have been shot. But in all that time, I missed the central point."

Vince looked up from his shoes, wet lines on his cheeks.

"Dad was the one who put the gun there, and he was the one who loaded it. Ultimately, he was the one responsible for it and what happened because that gun was there. We were children and we didn't know crap. You thought the gun was a cool toy and were playing with it. You didn't mean to shoot Dad any more than I did. It happened." Peter stood up and walked over to his brother. "I'm so tired of feeling guilty about it." He looked at Luka. "I felt so bad for years that I thought I wasn't worthy of being loved."

"Is that why you were…," Vince began, but then he trailed off.

"I was lucky because Luka didn't buy my crap, and he figured he knew best, which he did. He ignored my protests and showed me that I couldn't let what happened to me when I was six dictate the rest of my life. And you have to do the same thing. Your daughters and wife deserve it. I think it's time we let it go, both of us."

"But I let everyone think you did it," Vince said.

"I was six years old. You were eight! It shouldn't have mattered to anyone who shot Dad. What was important was that there was a loaded gun around and we got our hands on it. We could have shot each other or ourselves. Mom should have understood that I was just a kid. Instead, she blamed me for what happened and hated me for it. She should have been forgiving and she wasn't. It took me twenty-five years to be able to begin forgiving myself for what happened, but I shouldn't have had to. Mom should have forgiven me a long time ago."

Vince lifted his gaze. "Mom," he began, and then his eyes widened. Peter could see a light go on in his eyes as something clicked into place. "She never treated me any better than you."

Peter sighed. "Mom has always blamed me for what happened. After Dad died, she stopped paying much attention. She withdrew, and I always felt alone." His throat tightened. He'd told himself he wouldn't do this, but tears filled his eyes. "I always felt alone after that. Mom blamed me for what happened and never forgave me for it." Peter took a gasping breath and then felt Luka's familiar touch on his shoulder. "The worst part was I never forgave myself either." Peter wiped his eyes.

"What do you want me to do?" Vince asked.

"There's nothing either of us can do. What happened is over." Peter heaved a huge breath, filling his lungs. "I think I needed to talk to someone who might know what I was feeling. Except for the one time when we were kids, we never spoke about what happened." Peter swallowed and moved back to his chair. Luka sat on the arm next to him, resting his hand on Peter's. With that small touch, Peter knew everything was going to be okay. "After meeting with the doctor and realizing what had happened, my first instinct was to confront the entire family and set the record straight. I hadn't done this... thing... I thought I had. Vindicate myself." Peter motioned grandly. "But the doctor and Luka both told me to think about what I was going to do and what I wanted. Over the next few days I slowly, almost painfully, began to realize that I wasn't alone. That you had gone through the same things I had, just as silently and probably with just as much pain. So I came here to clear the air and to...." Peter shook his head. "I don't know, it might sound wrong, and I mean it in the best way possible, to say that I forgive you."

Vince stared at him and said nothing, his expression unreadable. He didn't move, and Peter wondered what would happen next. In bed the night before, he'd rehearsed Vince yelling and denying everything. He'd imagined acceptance and then tears. He'd even imagined Vince trying to convince him that his now clear memories were wrong, but he'd never imagined total silence.

After what seemed like a very long time, Vince set down his beer bottle and stood up. Thinking it was a dismissal, Peter stood as well, turning toward Luka and nodding toward the stairs. When he turned back to Vince to say good-bye, his brother stepped to him, extended his arms, and hugged him. Peter's older brother held him close. It took Peter a few seconds to realize that Vince was crying. He hadn't seen his brother cry about anything since his father's funeral. Tears welled in Peter's eyes. "It's all right. We both need to forgive and let it go." Peter held his brother tightly. "We were children, and it was an accident."

"Are you boys okay?" Margaret asked from the top of the stairs.

"Yes," Vince answered her. He stepped back and wiped his eyes. "I don't know what to say, little brother."

"How about saying nothing and letting it go?" Peter offered. He knew what had happened and was determined to go on with his life, guilt-free. "There's been enough recrimination to last a lifetime."

Vince wiped his eyes and nodded.

"I promised Mom I'd go see her."

A commotion from upstairs told all of them that the twins were up from their nap. Peter and Luka followed Vince up the stairs, and after diaper changes, they were each settled on the sofa with a baby and a bottle. Justine looked up at Luka with huge brown eyes, while she held one of his fingers in her tiny hand.

"Have you ever thought about having children?" Peter whispered to Luka, who shook his head.

"It not an option," Luka said. "Do you want babies?"

"I think so," Peter answered. "But not right away." Luka smiled at that answer and returned his attention to Justine, who seemed enthralled.

Once the girls were fed and burped, Margaret spread play mats on the floor, and they spent a while with them until the girls tired. Margaret and Vince each held one of the babies, who fell asleep in their arms. Peter and Luka each said good-bye to both of them and the babies before quietly leaving the house.

"That go very well, I think," Luka said.

"Yeah," Peter breathed, "it went very well." Better than he'd hoped. Now it was time to visit his mother. Peter wasn't sure if he should say anything at all to her. He'd had the truly important conversation. His mother would think and act the way she wanted.

They got in the car, and Peter drove to his mother's. When he entered, he found her sitting on the sofa. "How are you feeling?" he asked as he leaned down to kiss her cheek.

"I'm doing all right. I should get this patch off in a few days, and then I have to wear dark glasses for a while, but otherwise I'm fine." She reached up to Luka and took his hand.

"That's very good," Luka said, holding her hand for a few seconds and then releasing it.

"So it wasn't as bad as you thought?" Peter asked.

"No. I'll have the other one done as soon as this one is healed," she told him and settled back against some pillows. She motioned toward the chairs and they sat down.

"We were just at Vince's," Peter explained. "Luka and I fed the twins. They're getting so big."

"Children grow up so very fast," she said wistfully. "I remember when the three of you were young and your father took all of us camping." She smiled and Peter tried to remember. "We were on the other side of the lake, staying at one of the state parks. Your father had brought a tent and it was cold."

Peter chuckled. "I remember. It was cold, so I got up and held my clothes in front of the little heater to warm them up before I put them on."

"Yes. I thought you were going to turn blue because all you wore was some summer pajamas and your feet were bare. But you refused to put on the cold clothes. Eventually we got you dressed."

Peter nodded. "I remember Dad taking us out one afternoon to look for bullfrogs. We were walking around the edge of this pond, and Vince got too close to the water. I think he began to fall in because Dad reached for him, but he mustn't have had as good a footing as he thought, because they both fell into the slimy green water."

"You ran back to camp screaming that your daddy had been turned into a swamp monster," his mother said, smiling brightly for a few seconds. "He was so good with all you kids. After he was gone, I didn't know what to do. I had three kids, the oldest of which was eight. And to have him die that way." She paused and her expression shifted to the one Peter was used to: hard and cold. "I don't think this is a good subject for us to be discussing."

"Why not, Mom?" Peter pressed. "I've been seeing a psychologist so he can help me deal with what happened."

"That's good, I guess," she said with almost no feeling. "But nothing will change what happened, and there isn't anything that will bring him back."

"I know. But maybe we all need to forgive each other for what happened and the way we've treated each other. What happened to Dad was a long time ago, and you raised all of us the best you could." Peter decided he wouldn't say anything he didn't have to. Let his mother believe what she wanted.

"Forgive what? Shooting your father?" she asked, becoming very agitated.

"How about forgiving Dad," Peter countered, and his mother's eyes went wide. "He was the one who had a loaded gun sitting around. You always said you didn't want it in the house, so you told him to get rid of it. But he didn't. He hid it in his shed... and it was loaded. We thought it was a toy. We were children." Peter paused and glanced at Luka, who nodded encouragingly. "It isn't fair of you to have blamed us all these years for what happened when we were that young."

"Not fair?" his mother said. "I'll tell you what isn't fair. Your grandparents hated your father. They kept pushing me to marry the son of your grandfather's business partner. Jacob was a real weasel. I hated him, but they didn't care. Your father loved me and fought for me with your grandfather. He even threatened to take me away and marry me in another state if that was what I wanted." She calmed slightly. "It wasn't, and your father jumped through hoops and went through hell to get my parents to agree to the marriage. They did, of course. But after going through all that... for me... I knew he loved me more than anything. We got married, eventually started our family, and bought this house." She dabbed her eye with a tissue from the box beside the sofa. "Both of us had such dreams. We were going to raise you kids and then spend our retirement seeing the country."

"Dad was always talking about spending hours on the open road," Peter said, remembering one of his dad's bedtime stories.

"Yeah. Instead, someone broke into the Kleindinsts' house across the street, and your father was determined to protect us. He bought that damned gun, and when I wouldn't let him keep it in the house, he hid it out in the shed. Like that was going to do us any good. The only thing it did was get him killed by—" She stopped. "No, it wasn't fair. None of it was fair. Life sure as hell isn't fair."

Peter stood up and walked to the far side of the room, staring at the fireplace mantle with the picture of his father sitting front and center. He heard Luka walk up behind him.

"It's okay," Luka said.

Peter looked over his shoulder and sighed.

"What wasn't okay was you blaming us, blaming *me*, for Dad's death." He whirled around. Suddenly he had to get this out. "I was six and you blamed me because Dad was gone. After that you didn't care if I existed. I needed you more than anything, and you weren't there." He walked over to where his mother sat staring at him like he was from another planet. "I didn't shoot Dad."

His mother stared back at him, saying nothing. She opened her mouth and then closed it again. She knew. It was written in her eyes.

"Mother," he prompted. "That isn't a surprise to you, is it?"

She swallowed and said nothing.

"You knew. I didn't know until late last week. I spent all these years blaming myself for something I didn't do, and you knew all along. You... you...." Peter breathed deeply, inches from throttling her.

Instead he had to get out. Right now. He raced toward the front door and yanked it open hard enough that it hit the stop. He raced into the front yard, to the shade of one of the maple trees his father had planted, and gasped for fresh air. All these years of making him feel guilty every time she wanted anything had been a lie. She'd already known.

"Fuck!" He yelled up into the branches and thick leaves. He wondered if she'd pulled the same crap with Vince, making him feel guilty as well. Jesus, what a manipulative bitch.

He heard the front door open and snap closed. Luka walked out across the lawn and stood next to him.

"I think we can go now," Peter said. "There's nothing here."

Luka touched his shoulder. "Talk to her," he said.

"I can't right now." He turned to Luka. "All this time, she knew. She could have said something." His head felt like it was going to explode. The pressure behind his eyes built and built, and he knew he needed to calm down. Luka stepped in front of him.

"Close your eyes," Luka said.

Peter looked at him skeptically but did as he asked. He felt Luka's fingers on his temples, making small circular motions.

"That better?" Luka asked after a few seconds.

"Yes," Peter answered, tension draining from his head.

"Good," Luka said.

Peter opened his eyes as Luka looked back at him. "What?" he whispered.

"Maybe your mama not know that you do not know," Luka said.

Peter closed his eyes once again. This was too damned much. He was quickly coming to the conclusion that none of it was worth it. The baggage he kept carrying along with him was just too much. He opened his hands, relaxing his fingers, imagining a suitcase falling to the ground. He had to let it go, get rid of all of it. Peter took a deep breath, slowly released it, and then took another. Luka lowered his hands and Peter stood stock-still. Then slowly, he took a single step and another. The imaginary suitcase he'd dropped stayed right where it was. Peter took another step and another, walking toward his car.

"Let's go home," he said to Luka.

"What about your mother?" Luka asked when Peter stopped to open the car door.

"I know what I want now and I've let it go. Now it's her turn to decide what she wants." Peter looked toward the house. "When she's ready she'll let me know, and if she's never ready, I can deal with it now too." He pulled open the driver's door and got in the car. Thankfully, Luka didn't ask or say anything. He simply got in the car, and Peter started the engine and backed down the driveway.

They rode in silence until they got to Luka's. Peter parked and sat, staring out the windshield, seeing nothing.

"You okay?" Luka asked just above a whisper.

"Yes. For the first time in as long as I can remember, I'm fine." The sun was beginning to set, Bella's house casting a shadow over most of the backyard. "Would you like to go get something to eat?"

"You really okay?" Luka asked skeptically.

"Yes. I think so. I aired things out with Vince, and I hope we'll be good. And Mom, well, Mom is Mom. She knew what happened, and I believe she used my ignorance to her advantage, or tried to. But that doesn't matter. The ball's in her court now. I know what happened, and she now needs to decide what kind of relationship she wants to have. I don't need her any longer. I haven't for a long time."

Luka turned and looked at him strangely.

"It's not that I don't love my mother. But it's time our relationship changed. I don't need a mother any longer. And when I needed one, she wasn't there, or at least it didn't feel like it. So if she wants a relationship, then it has to be one of equals. And if she doesn't, I think I can live with that. I'm not going to bend over backward for her any longer." Peter flashed Luka a smile. "What I need isn't something my mother can give me." He reached over and cupped the back of Luka's head with his hand. "What I need is you.

I need to feel loved and cared for. You do that for me." Peter brought their lips together and kissed Luka.

"Should we go inside?" Luka asked.

"Yes," Peter answered softly. "I think making out in the car is something we're both a little old for." He followed Luka into the apartment and smiled when he saw all the organized paperwork sitting on the table. "Is everything going okay?"

"Yes. I have job people filling out the forms. They say they happy to do it for me," Luka said. He made a face and knew what he'd said wasn't exactly true. "They be done tomorrow and I can send everything." Nervousness crept into Luka's voice. Peter knew he was worried about what might happen. Peter was, as well, but they'd filled out everything they'd been asked to, and Luka had come here legally. He'd also followed all the rules and procedures, so Peter could only hope that it was only a matter of time before everything would be settled.

"I make dinner," Luka said and got to work. Peter had forgotten in all the excitement that they hadn't stopped to eat. As soon as Luka mentioned food, he was instantly starving. He helped make a quick and easy dinner of salad and some leftover sausages that tasted better the second day. After they ate, he helped Luka clean up, and then they settled in the living room on the sofa and watched television with Luka's legs stretched over Peter's lap.

This was heaven—someone to spend time with, watch television with, and be close to. The sex was great, but Peter knew a relationship was more than that. It was having someone to do nothing with. Someone who fulfilled and made him complete without having to have huge plans.

Peter rubbed Luka's feet, then pulled off his socks and stroked his foot and then up his leg. He let his hands wander, not breaking contact, but not pressing either. Luka was his and he belonged to Luka. When the character Sheldon on the television program said something ridiculous, Luka laughed, and Peter did the same.

"I understand this *Big Bang Theory*," Luka said. "I work with some of these people." Luka laughed again, and Peter smiled, truly happy—at least for the moment.

Chapter 10

A FEW weeks later, Luka was working quietly at his computer in the lab. He was afraid to start anything at this point. He couldn't concentrate very well, and he didn't want to chance messing up some of the delicate work that he had to complete. A soft knock sounded on the door, and he swiveled around in his chair.

"Peter," he said with a quick smile. "Why are you here?"

"You have an appointment at the immigration office, and I was coming to go down with you."

Luka nodded and swiveled back around. He closed his applications and shut down the computer before standing. He wasn't sure what he'd need, but he had brought copies of all of the paperwork he'd completed so far. "I'm ready to go," he said.

Peter smiled. "Your English keeps getting better and better."

"I have a good teacher," Luka said. Now that he'd been hearing almost nothing but English for a few months, it was getting easier. The words came to him, and he often didn't have to think so hard about them. There were times when they simply flowed rather than being translated to and from Serbian. He knew that was a good sign.

Luka got his bag and motioned Peter into the hallway. He locked up and walked with him out of the building. "Do you think we can go to Serbian Old Towne tonight for dinner?"

"Are you feeling a little homesick?" Peter inquired.

Luka nodded. The past week or two, he'd found himself wishing for some of the things he'd left behind. He knew his old home was closed to him. But it didn't stop him from looking for the familiar.

"You know it's normal when you live in a strange place to… sometimes become disillusioned. Nothing is the same as it was in Belgrade, not the food or the way people do things. It's okay if you even feel angry about it sometimes."

Luka swallowed. "I did not want you to think I was angry at you."

Peter shook his head. "We'll go to the Serbian restaurant, and you can eat your fill and listen to the music and talk to people. It's okay to talk to me about feeling homesick and about being angry or frustrated."

"Mostly I am nervous about this meeting," Luka said. The caseworker had called to arrange the appointment, but hadn't been forthcoming about the purpose other than to explain that he needed to speak with Luka in person. Since that call two days earlier, Luka had been on pins and needles, wondering how long he would be able to stay. Peter had consulted with some of the people he worked with, and they had said Luka should be fine, but they also said immigration law was convoluted and could be difficult to navigate.

"Don't be. You have friends, and we're all here to support you," Peter said, but Luka could tell he was anxious as well. They hadn't talked much about those feelings, ones that had been ever present over the past few weeks, increasing a lot in the past few days. Luka kept having the feeling that this was it: his future would be decided based upon this meeting.

"I know, but I keep thinking about what will happen if they send me home," Luka said. He nearly stumbled as they left the building and walked across campus to where Peter had parked his car. They got in, and Peter drove across town through heavy traffic to the federal building. He parked on the street, and Luka got out, his gaze sliding up the glass-enclosed building. It appeared cold, and Luka shivered slightly.

"Let's go inside and find out what's happening," Peter suggested.

Luka didn't move right away.

"Think about it this way. Knowing one way or the other is better than all this wondering." Peter motioned him toward the door of the building, and they went inside.

Luka couldn't help looking up into the cavernous building while Peter spoke with the man behind the desk.

"It's on the sixth floor," he told Luka.

They went to the elevator and rode up with Luka watching the numbers change on the display. When the doors opened, they got out and entered an office.

"I have appointment with Marvin Weston," Luka told the receptionist. "I'm Luka Krachek."

"Yes. I'll call and tell him you're here. Please have a seat. It should be just a moment."

"Thank you," Luka said and sat on the edge of one of the chairs. He kept glancing at the door and then at Peter, wondering what was in store for him. After a few minutes, the door opened and a man younger than him strode over to where he sat.

"Mr. Krachek, I'm Marvin Weston." He held out his hand. "It's very nice to meet you. Please follow me to my office, and we can review your case."

"This is Peter Montgomery." Luka turned to Peter and wondered how he should describe their relationship.

"I'm Luka's partner," Peter said, and Marvin smiled.

"Then this affects you as well," Marvin said. They walked through the doors and down a sparkling tiled hallway to a small office with a desk and two chairs. "Please have a seat."

"Do you usually meet directly with people like this?" Peter asked as he sat down.

"No. Usually decisions are made and letters sent, but this was a unique case that required additional scrutiny because of Mr. Krachek's cousin's death." Marvin sat down, and Luka and Peter did as well. "At first a number of us were a little baffled as to what to do, but you provided the information we needed in your application for lawful permanent residency. And the Serbian government added weight to your case."

"They did?" Luka asked.

"They contacted Luka and were watching his house at one point," Peter said.

"Yes, they were apparently very insistent in certain circles. But like I said, that helped us with our decision. Your sponsor being dead created a dilemma, but since you have employment and were already here, that worked in your favor as well."

"So I can stay?" Luka asked.

"Yes, you can stay," Marvin said. "We've decided to classify you as a refugee until your request for permanent residency is processed. It's a technicality, but it fits under the law because of the anticipated persecution that would result from you returning to Serbia. That seemed like the easiest fit. I'm recommending the approval of your application for permanent residency, so you should get your green card in the mail in a few weeks. Once that happens, you'll be able to apply for citizenship in five years, if that's what you wish."

Luka leaned forward. "I can stay?" he repeated.

Marvin smiled broadly. "Yes. You can stay."

"I don't want to be mean or anything, but you could have told him over the phone," Peter said.

Marvin nodded. "I probably could have. But I spend my days telling people no, I need this paperwork completed, or this is wrong. I had some good news for once, and I wanted to be able to share it in person. One of the best parts of my job is times like this. Also, I wanted Mr. Krachek to understand everything that is happening. And that if he is in any way bothered by anyone from the Serbian government, he is to call the police. The Serbian government has been notified that their presence in this matter is not welcome." Marvin paused. "You have skills that will benefit this country. That was obvious from the recommendations we received from the university. It's a pleasure to welcome you to the United States." Marvin stood up and shook Luka's hand. "If I need anything more I will be in contact, but I think we simply need to wait now."

"Thank you," Luka said, shaking Marvin's hand vigorously and then stepping back. He still held the portfolio of papers.

Peter and Marvin shook hands as well, and then Peter and Luka left the office. Luka made it to the elevator and waited until the doors slid closed before yelling his relief and happiness. Then he kissed Peter hard, practically trying to climb him, and only backed away when the elevator stopped.

When the doors opened, Luka sheepishly stepped out and hurried toward the doors to the building with the portfolio strategically held in front of him so he didn't give everyone in the lobby an eyeful. When they made it to the car, Peter was still smiling. They hurriedly drove to Luka's. Luka got out and grinned at Peter over the top of the car. Peter smiled back and looked toward the door with a "let's hurry up" look. Peter's smile faded, and Luka wondered what was up until he followed Peter's gaze.

Peter's mother sat on the swing in the backyard. She stood up and approached as they walked toward her.

"What are you doing here?" Peter asked.

"Luka told me where he lived when we were talking, and since you weren't at your place, I took the chance that you were here and drove myself. I parked on the street out front. Your friend Bella said you would most likely come back here and that I could wait if I wanted."

Luka unlocked the door. "You can come in if you like," he said.

Peter stopped her. "What are you doing here? You could have called if you wanted to talk to me."

"No, I don't think I could," she said before turning to Luka. "Thank you. That's very nice." She stepped inside, and Luka shrugged before following her. Peter came as well. Luka got both of them to sit in the living room and went to get drinks. He wasn't sure what to serve, but pulled out a bottle of slivovitz just in case. He had some lemonade in the refrigerator and brought that to start with, along with three glasses.

Peter sat on the sofa, his mother in the chair, both staring at each other. Luka poured the glasses and handed one to each of them. He sat next to Peter and waited for one of them to break the ice.

"What did you want to say, Mom?" Peter finally asked. "You came all this way."

She took a sip from her glass. "I know you blame me for a lot of things," she began.

"Mom, growing up I felt as though I didn't exist much of the time. I thought you hated me because of what I thought I'd done to Dad. Now I find out that I didn't shoot Dad and that you knew but didn't tell me, or even talk about it with me." Peter set his glass on the table without drinking from it. "I daresay Vince felt much the same way. We were left on our own."

"Your father was dead, and I was lost too," she said.

"Yeah, well, you were an adult—we were children who needed you."

Peter's mother reached for a tissue, and Luka wondered what was coming next. She wiped her eyes and sniffed. "Vince told me years ago what happened, and I should have said something, but I didn't realize…."

Peter turned toward him, and Luka gently patted his leg. He knew this was hard for Peter, but Luka thought this was a conversation they both needed to have.

"What happened to Dad was an accident. Yes, Vince and I had been playing with the gun, but we had no idea it was loaded, and when the gun went off…." Peter could still see his father's chest covered with blood. He would probably remember that image for as long as he lived. "But Mom, the only one responsible for Dad's death is Dad. He was the one who kept the loaded gun." Peter saw his mother begin to cry.

"I've been alone for a very long time, and I'm going to die alone," she whispered.

"Mom!" Peter snapped, and Luka started in surprise at the tone. "Believe it or not, this isn't about you. It's about me and Vince. You made us feel guilty for what happened and then checked out. We all needed you, but the only one you seemed to be there for was Julie." Peter paused and took a deep breath, his tone softening. "Look, all that is over. Vince and I are both grown-ups. Vince has a wife and two beautiful daughters. I have Luka and am moving on with my life."

"So you don't need me anymore?" Peter's mother asked, just shy of tears.

"That's the problem, Mom. We haven't needed you for a long time. When you checked out, we couldn't rely on you anyway." Peter paused, and Luka nodded when he glanced at him. He had to go on and see this through. So Luka encouraged him. "Do you remember in high school when I was in the choir and we went on that trip to Washington, DC?"

"Yes. You had the best time, and I gave you permission to go." She sounded pleased.

"I did have a great time. But what you didn't know was that the trip cost three hundred dollars and what you don't remember was me mowing every lawn in the neighborhood the entire summer so I could pay for it. I never asked you for the money because I never thought to do that. Even in high school I didn't need you for most things. You'd checked out long before that as far as I was concerned, so I became very self-sufficient. I paid my own way through college, and I'm still paying for it." Peter leaned closer to his mother. "The point I'm making is that I don't need you any longer and haven't in a while. So you have to decide the kind of relationship you want. I'm fine with visiting you on the occasional holidays and seeing you when I get time. But now my life is my own. I've earned that. I'm not going to drop what I'm doing to help you any longer. If you want something, then ask, but don't presume an answer."

"So I'm not your mother anymore." She stood up. "I raised you and gave you a place to live. I cared for you and fed you and...."

"Let me lead a life filled with guilt in order for you to remain in control," Peter said. "So like I was about to say, the past is the past and I forgive you for everything. You are my mother and I do love you. But our relationship from here on out will be based upon mutual respect. So if you want to be close, then it will have to be as equals. As friends, if you will. Because, Mom, there's nothing left at this point."

"Is that what you meant the other week?" she asked, dabbing her eyes.

"Yes. I'm still your son, and you're my mother. But if you want a relationship going forward, then it needs to be on a different basis than the one we've had. Not based on the guilt I carried with me for twenty-five years." Peter stood up and walked over to her. "Mom, this is what I need right now. I can't do things based upon guilt any longer, and neither can Vince." He took her hand. "You need to forgive both of us for what happened... and forgive Dad."

Her lower lip quivered, and Peter knew he might have hit on something important. "All this time we've all assessed blame and carried guilt over what happened when Vince and I were kids. But it needs to end, for Vince, for you, for me, and for Julie. We all need to move on and forgive each other. Otherwise you'll never be able to move on, and Julie will end up like you."

She gasped, and Luka stood up and quietly left the room. The two of them needed some time alone. In the kitchen, Luka grabbed the bottle of slivovitz and three small glasses. When he returned to the living room, they weren't talking, just sitting.

"In my family, when we fight and make up, we settle it with a drink," Luka said. He set the glasses on the coffee table and poured three shots. He handed one to Peter and another to his mother. "Mothers and sons sometimes fight," Luka said. "But in the end you are family, and that is more important." Luka hoped he got the words right. So instead of talking, he lifted his glass and downed the liquor. Peter did the same, and then Peter's mother lifted the glass but looked like she didn't know what to do.

"Belt it, Mom," Peter said. She lifted the glass and drank it all. Her eyes widened and she gasped.

"You want another?" Luka asked, lifting the bottle.

She shook her head.

"Come on, Mom," Peter said.

Luka poured a second round. They all drank and then set down their glasses, inhaling deeply.

"That better," Luka said, smiling. "Today I get good news." He was trying to change the subject. Luka wasn't sure it would work, but he gave it a try. "I find out that I get to stay."

"Yeah, Mom," Peter said. "We just met with the immigration service, and the short version is that Luka is going to get his green card and will be able to stay."

"That's wonderful," she said, her eyes rolling a little, probably from the alcohol. "You make Peter happy, and that's what every mother loves to see." She picked up the glass of lemonade and took a large drink. Peter stared open-mouthed at her.

"We are going to dinner to celebrate," Luka said. "We have Serbian food. You come with us." He wasn't sure how Peter would react, but today felt more and more like a party to him. He would get to stay in this country, Peter and his mama were talking to each other, and…. "I get Bella too," he said and got up. He hurried across the lawn and knocked on the back door.

Bella answered it. "You've been drinking," she observed almost as soon as she opened the door.

"Just slivovitz with Peter's mama. We go to dinner and we like you to come too. We celebrate that I get to stay." Luka grinned.

"Okay, but I'll drive. I'm the only one that hasn't been drinking." She sounded almost as excited as Luka felt, and her smile was wonderful to see.

"Okay. We be ready soon," Luka said.

"Fine. I'll get ready, and you can meet me out front in ten minutes."

Luka agreed and hurried back. Peter and his mother were talking. The alcohol had probably smoothed the way. "We ready in ten minutes," he said. He thought about offering another shot to each of them, but put the bottle away instead. He wanted them lubricated, not drunk.

"What's Serbian food like?" Marie asked a few minutes later as they walked across the lawn and out to the front.

"It's wild and spicy, like me," Luka said and then realized how he must have sounded.

"You'll love it, Mom," Peter said as Bella joined them.

They got in the car, and Bella drove them to Serbian Old Towne while Peter called to let them know they were on the way. By the time they arrived, Luka was in high spirits. The music in the restaurant reminded him of home, as did the scents coming from the kitchen. They were shown to a table, and Luka ordered appetizers. He was anxious, hungry, and happy.

"So," Bella began when the conversation seemed to stall from the beginning.

"Bella's going to have a baby," Luka said.

Instantly Marie perked up. "When are you due?" Marie asked.

"Mid-February. I'm only a few months along, but I'm very excited." Bella swallowed, and Luka instantly regretted bring up the subject.

"Mom," Peter said. "Bella lost her husband a few months ago, and…."

Marie reached out to Bella, who was sitting next to her, and took her hand. "I know what you're going through. I really do. It's hard at first, but you'll have a piece of your husband that no one can take away. When I lost my husband, I didn't realize that. In fact, I didn't realize that until recently."

Luka turned to Peter, nodding slowly. Under the table, he found Peter's hand and slid their fingers together. Peter smiled at him, and Luka knew what his mother had said was what Peter needed to hear.

"Who will be with you when the time comes?"

Bella sniffled. "My sister, most likely." She looked at Luka, who nodded. "I'd like it if Luka would be there was well. He's family, and I want my child to have a father. Peter and Luka have been there for me, and I'd be pleased if they'd be in his or her life."

Luka smiled at her. "Of course we be there." He hoped he wasn't out of line speaking for Peter, but the slight squeeze of his hand told him he was just fine.

Their server came, and they ordered drinks and then dinner. Marie wasn't sure what to order, but Bella explained everything. They ended up ordering multiple dishes that got shared around the table so Marie could taste some of everything: the buttery, crispy burek; savory, spicy cevaps; tart olives; and mellow peppers. All of it reminded Luka of home and was just what he needed.

"This is wonderful," Marie said more than once during the meal. "Can you make this?" she asked at one point before taking another bite of the flaky-crusted burek. She was looking at Bella, but Luka answered.

"Yes, I can. My mother used to make them all the time. They were a favorite in our house." Luka tried not to get too sentimental. "My mother was very traditional and did not think her son need to know how to cook, but my grandmother was practical. So she convinced my mother that I need to be able to cook if I am on my own. My mother teached me, and I think she liked having me help."

"I think if I ate like this every day, I would weigh a great deal," Marie said. "But I think I'd be happy."

"I am glad you like it," Luka said. Then he raised his glass, and the others did the same. "I want to drink to my new home with my new friends and family," Luka said. He lightly bumped Peter's shoulder, and Peter did the same thing in return. Then they all drank and continued the meal.

By the time they were finished, all the plates had been cleaned. Luka felt like he'd had a visit home, and Bella appeared stuffed and happy. Even Marie was smiling. Luka paid the check when it was time, and they all got up to leave. Bella took Luka's arm and led him toward the car.

"They need a few minutes to talk," Bella said. Luka had already gotten that idea, and he went with Bella to the car ahead of Peter and his mother.

"Did you mean what you said... about your baby?" Luka asked.

"Yes. I want my baby to know his Uncle Luka and his Uncle Peter." She paused for a few seconds. "You know it was a very nice thing you did for Peter and his mother. And don't tell me you weren't trying to do anything, because I know better. You got them to come to dinner so they could do something fun together."

Luka shrugged.

"You're such a softie," she said.

"I am not," he countered, looking over to where Peter and his mother were talking. "They just needed some time when they weren't mad at each other."

Bella nodded, and they watched as Peter and his mother walked together toward the car. They both had smiles on their faces. Well, maybe not smiles, but they weren't scowling and didn't appear angry. Bella unlocked the car, and they all got inside. Marie sat in the front, and Luka sat in back. Peter took his hand once the doors were closed and they started to move. Luka half listened as Marie spoke with Bella about the trials and joys of motherhood while he scooted closer to Peter and enjoyed being with him. Luka had had enough drama, worry, and excitement to last him the rest of his life.

When they arrived, Bella parked, and everyone got out. Peter's mother said good night and got ready to leave.

"I thought you couldn't drive," Peter said as his mother walked toward her car.

"I got the okay. They took care of the worst eye, and as long as I'm careful, I'm fine. In a few weeks they'll do the other eye and I won't be able to drive again for a while, so I'm enjoying the freedom while I have it." She stepped closer to Peter.

Luka turned away. Bella was already heading up the walk. Luka knew he should do the same, but he wanted to hear what they said.

"Can you ever find it in your heart to forgive me?"

After about ten seconds, Luka headed up the walk, but when he turned, he saw Peter hug his mother, and then she walked to her car and got inside as Peter walked toward him. Luka stood next to Peter and watched her drive away. Then they both strolled through the yard hand in hand back toward his apartment.

Inside, Luka didn't let go of Peter's hand and led him into the living room. They sat on the sofa. Luka pulled Peter to him, kissing him, and nipped at his lips.

"There are so many times when I wonder what I did to deserve you," Peter said.

Luka stroked Peter's stubble-rough cheek. "We do nothing. That is what make love so special. We all do nothing to get it and it make us all very happy. I did not do anything, and you did not do anything. Love just happens."

"Sometimes I think you're a philosopher rather than a scientist," Peter said with a smile.

Luka moved closer and proceeded to kiss away the smile and the rest of what Peter was going to say. As they kissed, their passion built quickly.

They moved upstairs, their clothes seeming to melt away. Luka pressed Peter back onto the bed and climbed on top of him. Skin to skin, lips to lips, he reveled in each touch. Luka's entire body tingled with each of Peter's caresses.

"You're mine, Luka," Peter whispered between kisses. "I want you to be my one and only forever. I know you still love Misha, but I hope you can love me the way you loved him."

Luka stilled, gazing down into Peter's eyes. "I will never love you the way I loved Misha. I can't. But I love you for you. He was different."

"Oh," Peter breathed, stilling.

"It not that way. I love you for you. I not love you the way I love Misha because Misha was Misha and you are you." He leaned closer to Peter. "I love you, Peter. I love you for you. Not like Misha. I love you like Peter." He really hoped he was making sense. It was hard for him to explain the contents of his heart. He didn't have the words in either English or Serbian, so instead he proceeded to show Peter.

Luka caressed, licked, and kissed every inch of Peter's body until he was breathless and begging Luka for more. Luka listened and continued driving Peter out of his mind. "I show you how much I love you."

"I think I understand," Peter said, gasping for air.

"No. Not yet," Luka whispered as he reached to the nightstand. He got the supplies and prepared both of them before straddling Peter's hips and sinking down onto him. "Misha is past; you are future," Luka said, gritting his teeth as Peter filled him. "You are who I want in my life."

"And I want you," Peter told him, grasping Luka's sides. "I want only you forever."

"You have me," Luka said. He leaned forward and kissed Peter. They moved together in near perfect harmony. Their mouths hung open and they gasped for breath as their passion took over. Luka rolled his hips and drove Peter wild, second after second, minute after minute. He prolonged the culmination of their love for as long as he could, until neither of them could contain it any longer. They climaxed together, shouting their release until the walls echoed it back to them. Luka didn't want to let Peter go, and once their bodies separated, they held each other, whispering their love into the darkness.

They made love for hours, celebrating their love and what Luka hoped was a real relationship well into the night. Finally, well after dark, tired and drained, Peter settled next to Luka. The words Luka heard before drifting into an exhausted sleep were "I love you." Luka muttered his response just before exhaustion claimed him, and they both slept.

Epilogue

"LUKA!" HE heard Peter call up the stairs of the small house he and Peter had started renting together a few weeks before Christmas. In November they had each asked the other if they wanted to move in. Since both their places were small, they decided to find a house they could rent. And three months later things were wonderful.

"What is it?" Luka called back as he finished buttoning his shirt. He'd gotten home from work a few minutes earlier and was changing into warm clothes before heading outside to shovel the walks.

"Your phone. It's Bella's sister," Peter said as he strode into the room. "She's gone into labor. Sima says that Bella is moving quickly and could deliver anytime."

Luka moved faster, fastened the final button, and pulled on his shoes. Then he hurried past Peter and grabbed his wallet and keys from the dresser. He followed Peter down the stairs and got his coat, hat, and gloves. He pulled them on, and the two of them left the house. He locked the door behind them and would have ended up on his back in the snow if Peter hadn't steadied him.

"Take it easy. We'll get there," Peter told him gently. "I don't want anything to happen to you."

They got to the car, and Peter hurried around to the driver's side. Luka huffed. He'd gotten his license a few months earlier, but Peter said he was a menace on the road.

"You can drive when it isn't quite so slippery."

"Fine," Luka said and slid into the passenger seat. He hadn't gotten a car of his own yet, but he was planning to buy one in the spring. Luka closed the car door, and Peter started the engine. Things in Luka's life—in *their* lives—had worked out remarkably well. He'd gotten his green card and his research was progressing very well. He and one of his colleagues were working on a paper together that could put the work they'd been doing on the academic and scientific map. He hadn't had any more visitors from the Serbian government, and he planned to apply to become a citizen as soon as he was able.

Peter pulled out into traffic, and Luka rested his gloved hand on Peter's leg. "Bella is going to be fine. All of the tests have come back good, with no signs of what the doctor originally feared."

"I know. I do not want her to be alone. We promise we be there for her," Luka said, filled with nervous excitement.

"We will be," Peter said and pulled out onto the street. They didn't seem to be moving very fast, and with each passing second Luka got a little more nervous.

Peter's phone rang, and he handed it to Luka.

"Hello," Luka said. "This is Peter's phone."

"Luka, it's Marie. I was calling to see if you and Peter would like to come to dinner on Saturday." The relationship between Peter and his mother had changed slowly as far as Luka could see. They both seemed to be finding their way.

"That would be very nice. We are on our way to the hospital now. Bella is having her baby." Luka couldn't help smiling.

"Give her my best," Marie said.

"I will, and I will have Peter call when we get to hospital," Luka said.

"Tomorrow is fine," Marie replied.

Luka said good-bye and hung up. He stared out the windshield as the snow continued coming down. There were times when it was hard to see anything but the lights of the car in front of them. Finally, to Luka's relief, Peter turned off the road and parked.

"I glad I not drive," Luka mumbled as he got out of the car and stepped carefully to avoid a pile of slush. He closed the car door, and they walked across the parking lot, dodging the truck removing the snow. Inside, the warmth was nearly overpowering, and he shoved his hat and gloves into his pockets, then opened his coat so he didn't get too warm. Peter spoke to someone behind the desk.

"She's this way," Peter said, and they hurried to an elevator and up to the second floor. In the delivery area, they checked in and were told that Bella was already in with her sister. "We're on the list," Peter explained, and she looked further.

"Yes, you are," she said. Luka didn't know what it meant, but it seemed to unlock the gate to information. "Bella is in delivery. At last report she was in active delivery, which means she's giving birth now. It says you're both allowed in the delivery room, but it's too late for that now. We will get you scrubbed and gowned so you can see her as soon as the baby is born."

She led them to a room where they washed and put on gowns, hats, masks, and covers for their shoes. When they were done, Luka and Peter followed the nurse, now dressed the same way, down a hallway. She peered inside a small window and then motioned for them to come forward. Slowly, Luka pushed the door open and then stepped into the delivery room.

Bella lay on a gurney, looking exhausted, with a small bundle in her arms. She smiled at them, and Luka stepped over to the bed and got a look at the tiny bundle.

"It's a boy," Bella said.

Luka smiled at her and then at Sima, who was standing off to the side.

"Are you going to call him Josif after his dad?" Luka asked.

Bella looked to Sima, who smiled and lightly patted her sister's shoulder. "Yes. We decided to call him Lucas Joseph," Bella said. "I want him to have an American name, so we decided to name him after you. We'll call him Lucas so there won't be any confusion when he's around his uncles." Bella eyes shone as she looked at the two of them.

Bella carefully lifted Lucas so Luka could hold him. He took the small sleeping bundle. The baby's eyes were closed, and he moved a little in his sleep. Luka rocked him slowly, unable to stop the tears as he thought how much Josif would love this and how unfair it was that he wasn't here to hold his son. *I take care of him for you*, Luka thought.

Peter moved closer, looking over Luka's shoulder, and little Lucas opened his eyes. The lights were dim, and Luka got a good peek into his eyes. His heart was gone, lost once again to a gorgeous man with dark eyes. Luka shifted slightly so Peter could get a better look. "He is beautiful, Bella."

"Just like his mother," Peter whispered. Luka nodded, but couldn't take his eyes off the sweet bundle he held. Lucas opened his mouth and began to cry softly. Luka settled him back in his mother's embrace.

"We're going to take both of them to a room," one of the nurses said. "You can meet them in room 212 in a few minutes."

Peter patted him on the shoulder, and after taking another look at Bella and the baby, they left the room.

After changing out of the sanitary gear, they walked to the room the nurse had described and sat down. Bella was wheeled in, and the nurse drew the curtain partway.

"He's hungry," the nurse said. Luka looked to Peter briefly, expecting to see a bottle. The nurse stepped around and helped Bella put the baby into the proper position. Both he and Peter looked away as Bella breast-fed Lucas for the first time.

"It's okay, boys," Bella said. "If you're going to be around for the next few months, you better get used to the tatas."

"Sorry, dear," Peter said. "But that's not going to happen."

"Breast-feeding is important," the nurse said. "It helps mother and baby bond, and it helps Bella impart some of her immunity to the baby." She looked on, and Luka hazarded a look. There was nothing to really see, other than Bella holding Lucas close, and he relaxed.

Sima came in, and Luka got up so she could sit down, but she shook her head. "I think you're both in good hands. I'm going to go home and get some rest." She leaned over the bed and kissed Bella's cheek. "Call if you need anything. Mom is trying to get here from

Chicago, but the weather has her stymied for now. But you know that won't keep her away for long. So get some rest—you'll need it." She said good-bye and left the room.

After a few minutes, Bella rearranged her gown and resettled Lucas. "Would you like to hold him?" she asked Peter.

He stepped forward and cradled Lucas in his arms. "Lucas, I'm your Uncle Peter," he said, rocking slightly. "You may not know it, but you're the luckiest little boy around. You got the world's best mommy. I know your daddy's with the angels, but he's looking down on you and he'll watch over you."

Luka felt tears forming in his eyes and didn't dare look at Bella.

"You've also got your Uncle Luka. He's one of the best people I know. Yes, he is," Peter added in baby talk. "You can sleep if you want, but I gotta tell you, your Uncle Luka is special." Peter turned, and their gazes locked. "See, he believed in me when I didn't believe in myself." Peter paused. "That's it. Stretch it out," Peter whispered to Lucas. "Yes." Lucas continued moving and then settled down. "Now, where was I?" Peter asked. "Oh, yeah, see, not everyone gets an Uncle Luka. And not everyone has people who will love you always, but your uncles will. I promise." Peter looked at Luka. "Unconditionally and for always. No matter what happens, what you do, or even if you turn into a Republican."

"Don't let his grandpa hear you say that," Bella said with a slight chuckle.

"That will be our little secret," Peter said, and then he slowly settled Lucas next to Bella. "I think it's time for Mama and Baby to get some rest."

"Are you leaving?" Bella asked.

"No," Peter said. "We'll be right here. You close your eyes and take a nap while Lucas is quiet. He'll need to eat again soon." Peter moved his chair next to Luka's and sat down. Without really thinking about it, Luka took Peter's hand. Peter leaned slightly against Luka's shoulder. "Maybe we should think about having a child."

"Maybe, eventually, but let's be uncles first."

Peter nodded and relaxed against him. The room grew quiet and soon Bella fell asleep.

"Volim te," Luka whispered to Peter, who tightened the grip on his hand.

"I love you too," Peter told him just as quietly.

Luka turned his head slightly and saw a world of meaning in Peter's eyes. Luka lifted Peter's hand to his lips and lightly kissed the back of it.

"My heart is light and happy, and that's because of you," Peter whispered in Luka's ear.

Luka was about to shake his head to protest, but didn't. Peter's heart was happy. It showed in almost everything he did, but especially in the way Peter now hummed to himself when he did things around the house. Luka was certain Peter didn't know he did it, and he had no intention of bringing it to Peter's attention. It was a sign to him that the baggage Peter had carried when they met was truly gone. His lover, partner, and friend was happy—as happy and contented as Luka was. That was all he could ask. They were building a life together, and some things were the same no matter where you lived. Being with someone took patience, communication, and compromise, just like it had in Belgrade. Things wouldn't be perfect.

Luka's leg cramped slightly, so he stood up and quietly walked toward the bed. Lucas was asleep, the picture of a tiny angel. Peter came up behind him, lightly touching his shoulder. Yes, things might not always be perfect, but moments of perfection, like this one, made it all worthwhile.

ANDREW GREY grew up in western Michigan with a father who loved to tell stories and a mother who loved to read them. Since then he has lived all over the country and traveled throughout the world. He has a master's degree from the University of Wisconsin-Milwaukee and works in information systems for a large corporation. Andrew's hobbies include collecting antiques, gardening, and leaving his dirty dishes anywhere but in the sink (particularly when writing). He considers himself blessed with an accepting family, fantastic friends, and the world's most supportive and loving partner. Andrew currently lives in beautiful historic Carlisle, Pennsylvania.

Visit Andrew's website at http://www.andrewgreybooks.com and blog at http://andrewgreybooks.livejournal.com/.

E-mail him at andrewgrey@comcast.net.

The Art Series from ANDREW GREY

The Bottled Up Series from ANDREW GREY

http://www.dreamspinnerpress.com

Love Means… Series from ANDREW GREY

Love Means… Series from ANDREW GREY

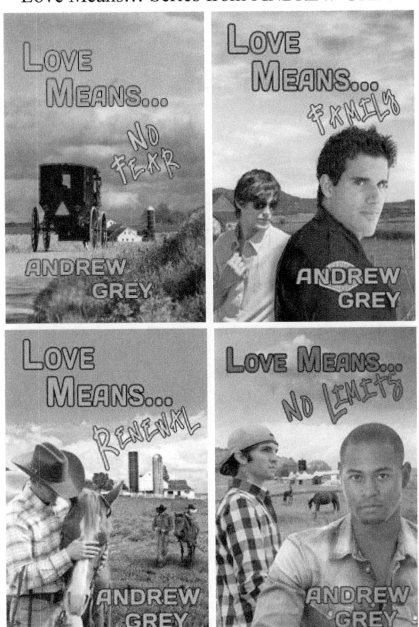

http://www.dreamspinnerpress.com

Taste of Love Stories from ANDREW GREY

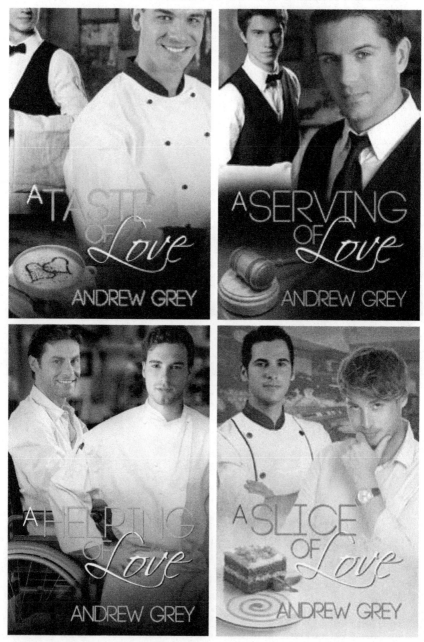

Children of Bacchus Stories from ANDREW GREY

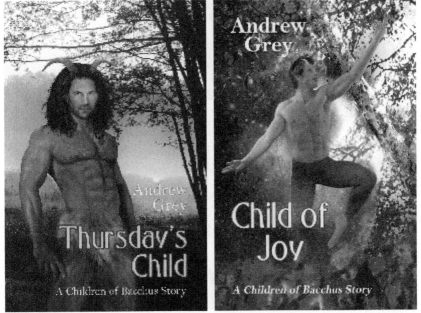

http://www.dreamspinnerpress.com

Good Fight Stories from ANDREW GREY

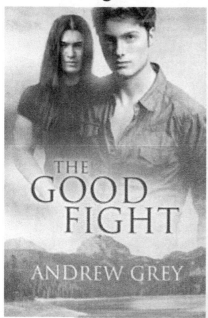

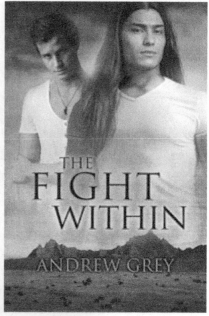

http://www.dreamspinnerpress.com

Stories from the Range from ANDREW GREY

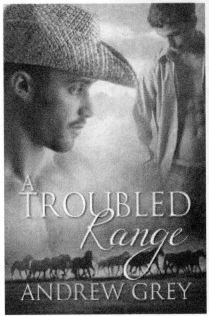

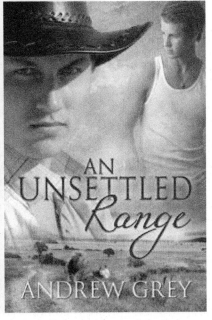

Stories from the Range from ANDREW GREY

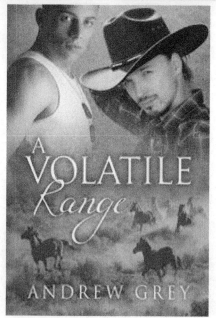

The Bullriders from ANDREW GREY

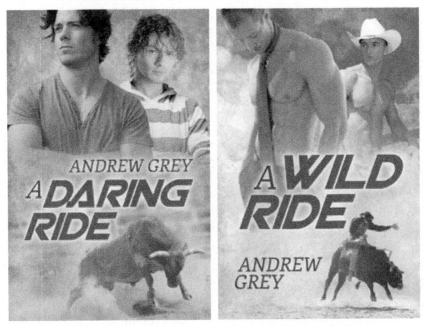

http://www.dreamspinnerpress.com

Senses Stories from ANDREW GREY

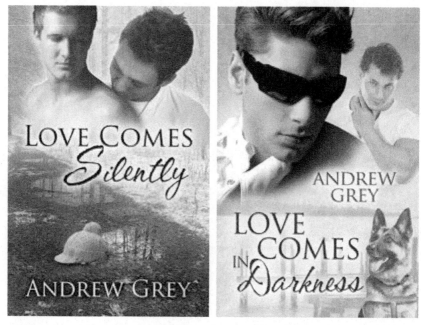

http://www.dreamspinnerpress.com

Seven Days Stories from ANDREW GREY

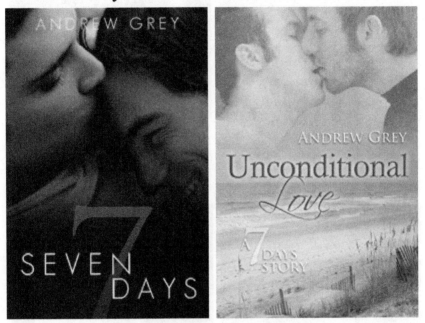

http://www.dreamspinnerpress.com

The Fire Series from ANDREW GREY

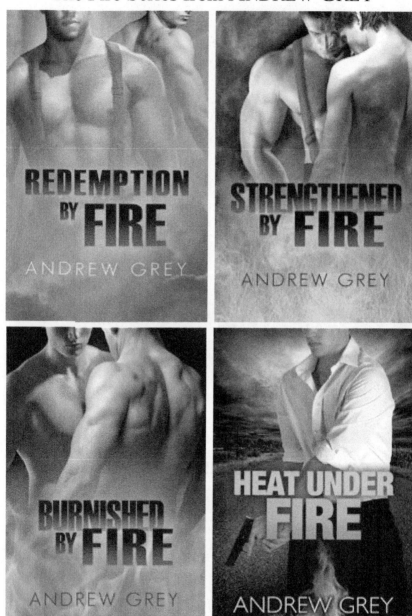

Work Out Series from ANDREW GREY

http://www.dreamspinnerpress.com

Work Out Series from ANDREW GREY

http://www.dreamspinnerpress.com

Children of Bacchus Stories from ANDREW GREY

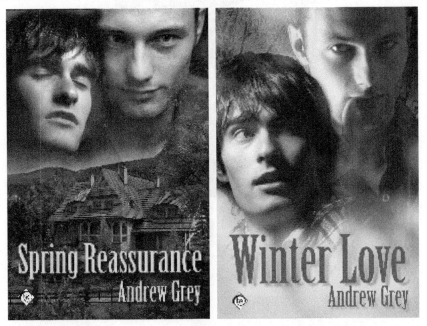

http://www.dreamspinnerpress.com

Also from ANDREW GREY

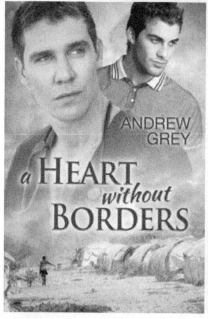

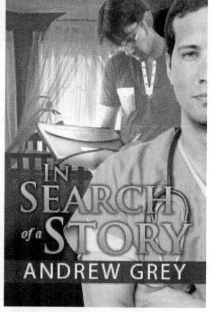

http://www.dreamspinnerpress.com

Also from ANDREW GREY

http://www.dreamspinnerpress.com

Also from ANDREW GREY

INSIDE
ANDREW GREY
OUT

Also from ANDREW GREY

ANDREW GREY

DUTCH Treat

Novellas from ANDREW GREY

http://www.dreamspinnerpress.com

Novellas from ANDREW GREY

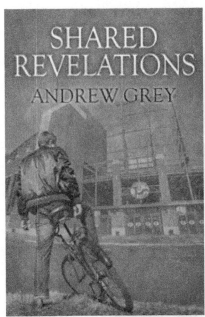

http://www.dreamspinnerpress.com